For Georgios Maragkos,
my Hammersmith Apollo.
πέφευγα· τἀληθὲς γὰρ ἰσχῦον τρέφω.

Jake Arnott

BLOOD RIVAL

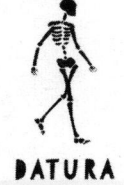

DATURA

DATURA BOOKS
An imprint of Watkins Media Ltd

Unit 11, Shepperton House
89-93 Shepperton Road
London N1 3DF
UK

daturabooks.com
I am taught by suffering to endure

A Datura Books paperback original, 2025

Copyright © Jake Arnott 2025

Edited by Daniel Culver and Travis Tynan
Cover by Mark Swan
Set in Meridien

ISBN 978 1 91741 514 9
Ebook ISBN 978 1 91741 515 6

Printed and bound in the United Kingdom by CPI Group (UK) Ltd, Croydon CR0 4YY

The manufacturer's authorised representative in the EU for product safety is eucomply OÜ – Pärnu mnt 139b-14, 11317 Tallinn, Estonia, hello@eucompliancepartner.com; www.eucompliancepartner.com

9 8 7 6 5 4 3 2 1

PART I

0

It happened at a place where three roads meet. Junction 1A of the M25, heading east towards Gravesend.

There's a killer on the road.

Just after dawn, on a bright June Sunday morning, Lee Royle was driving his dark-blue Land Rover Discovery home from a long night in Essex. He'd crossed the water at Dartford, idly dreaming of his ancient homeland. *Kent,* he mused as he changed down to ease into the slip road.

Then a red Mazda MX-5 roadster cut him up across the right-hand side, making his foot flinch sharply on the brake pedal. Lee raged and blared his horn. He flashed his headlamps full beam and gave chase, gaining on the impudent little sports car as they approached a roundabout at the foot of the slope.

As he overtook the MX-5, Lee glanced over to judge his tormentor. Just a kid. A boy racer. A baby driver. Royle caught the youth's eye and gazed a gorgon glare, but the kid just smiled back and gave him the finger. *Fucker,* Royle thought, and swerved around to block him off broadsides. The kid braked hard, his grin gritting as his head jerked back against the headrest.

For a moment, all was quiet but for the low drone of the motorway above and a light descant of birdsong from the embankment. Royle wondered if the dazed look in the kid's features was enough. He could drive off now, before the little bastard could recover his senses. But some impulse made him linger: That face. Something familiar about it.

And he knew then that he needed more. To humiliate him properly, give the boy a slap, if need be. Let baby driver know who was daddy. Just to make sure, he reached down beneath the driver's seat and pulled out the small sheath knife he kept there. He slipped it into the pocket of his zip-up jacket, opened the door and climbed out onto the road.

The kid was already out of his car and walking towards him. Again, Lee wondered if he knew him from somewhere. As he thought of all his enemies, Royle was glad he'd brought the blade with him. He stroked its outline gently through the cloth of his jacket as he turned to face his opponent.

"Get that fucking thing out of my way!" the kid called to him.

"What's your hurry, son?"

"Just move it!"

They closed in, circling each other in a lethal, courtly dance. Shaping up for combat.

"You want to watch yourself, sonny."

He said the words softly, and for a curious moment felt a caring tone in his heart. This was just a hot-headed young man, after all. Out of his depth.

"You don't know who I am," Lee warned him with a grim smile.

"Just fuck off out of my way," the kid spat out the words. "Old man."

Royle was in his late fifties but had kept himself in shape. His loose-limbed frame tensed at this taunt, his forearms raised slowly, instinctively. He stepped forward.

"Someone ought to teach you some manners," he said.

The kid bared his young chest and opened his arms in a beckoning gesture.

"Yeah?" he offered. "Come on then."

Royle's punch was intended to connect with the kid's chin and floor him in one, but he wasn't fast enough – age had softened him. The younger man saw it coming, ducked, and parried with his left, then came back under Lee's guard to deliver a sharp hook to the stomach. Royle doubled-up, winded, choking, desperately trying to find his footing. Then another fist smashed into his face, and he dropped down onto the tarmac.

He managed to roll away and scramble to his feet before the kid could land a kick. Squatting low, Royle could taste blood as he fumbled for the knife in his pocket. As the kid loomed over him, ready to strike once more, Lee showed him the blade.

"Want some of this?" he hissed, still out of breath.

Royle always relished that look of fear on an opponent's face. He'd never spent too much time dealing with the brutal end of things. He'd survived by knowing the odds. When you might make a killing, and when you might just have to walk away. And he'd prided himself on being utterly ruthless in business. Happy to let the others play at being the heavy. To cross the pavement, to do a bank or a security firm, while he'd be the one that managed the proceeds. Let the suckers take the risks and do the time; his eye was always on the profit. This was the key to his success with the Tunbridge Wells Cash Depot Robbery.

But there was business, and there was personal. And when the odds were right, he was never averse to taking somebody down. Especially if that somebody had tried to have him over.

And now this cocky little fucker was backing away, trying to hide the terror in his stupid face. Now was the moment. The moment that mattered.

Because he had proved he could do it, after all. He'd never been sure until that night, nearly twenty years ago. Never been sure if he was a killer or not until that night he found a man in his garden. The undercover cop spying on his house.

He'd been upstairs making love to his wife, Jo. It had been so powerfully primal that night. When he came, his whole being seemed to implode into darkness. Then, as he held her trembling body and caught his breath, he had heard the noise outside.

He'd let the dog out and taken a knife from the kitchen. He hadn't meant to kill the man. It was instinctive. He'd told the arresting officer: *You ask Ray Spinks; he'll tell you I'm not a cold-blooded killer.* But when the blood was up, he'd proved he could do it. And now, looking at the kid, he knew he could do it again.

He pointed the blade at the boy in a deliberate gesture of intent. But he was distracted by the look on the young man's face of in front of him.

"Please," the kid implored, his hands up, his eyes darting about, looking for a way out.

That look of fear usually made Royle feel bold. Powerful. But something else happened. He hesitated. Something about the young man's expression made him think of Jo, the argument that they had had the night before, and the dreadful thing he had made them do all those years ago.

An awful, paralysing sense of compassion took hold of him, and he felt his grip on the knife loosen. He lowered the blade; this might have been the most humane thing he had ever done in his life. It was almost an act of love.

And this moment of weakness was all the kid needed. He kicked the weapon out of Royle's hand and knocked him to the ground once again. Picking up the knife, he stood above the older man.

Lee looked up in horror as he suddenly realised what he recognised in his assailant. What he had feared all along. *No, he thought, it's not possible.*

The young man looked wild about the eyes, drugged up or in some kind of trance. And Lee's mind struggled with the awful truth. Of all the people that might want him dead – Ray Spinks, Chris Ipsworth, even his own wife – this was the one person in the world who had the right to truly hate him.

"Wait," he begged.

But the knife came down again and again.

As life's warmth bled out of him, Lee Royle thought of Jo once more. This was her revenge, perhaps, but what a curious way of taking it. With what Lee had always feared most: the killer inside. His blood rival.

The assailant walked back to his car. He looked around briefly, no traffic around or CCTV covering this slip road. This abrupt and impulsive act would be hidden from sight, even from himself. He could forget it now, pretend it never happened.

But as he drove away, he did not see the figure standing high up on the motorway embankment. The solitary witness who had watched it all happen.

1

Tucked away in the gently bucolic greenbelt of West Kent, Sevengates was a modern brick mansion with a colonnaded portico. At the front of the house stood an ornamental fountain, at the rear a large glass conservatory that opened onto a garden with raised beds and a small, enclosed orchard. Behind that was an outdoor pool, a tennis court, and a drive-in outbuilding large enough to keep two articulated lorries under complete cover.

The property could easily be missed by any traveller passing through that deceptively quiet part of the Home Counties. Seemingly off the beaten track, yet but a short drive from the badlands of South-East London. Right by the M20, which led to the busy ports of Folkestone and Dover, and close to its junction with the M25, the London Orbital Motorway.

And though carefully hidden away from prying eyes, every feature of Sevengates spoke of vigilance. Set on thirty acres of land encompassed by a high-perimeter fence, the property's entrance was barred by an ornate wrought-iron security gate. Beyond that, a copse of trees hid the property from the road, and a long, snaking driveway ensured that any approaching vehicle could be seen from the house long before it arrived.

As Detective Constable Meera Hussain and Family Liaison Officer Cheryl Symons made their slow, winding approach through the trees, they once again went through all the relevant details of the case, including what had happened since they first came to Sevengates to deliver the news of Lee Royle's killing.

"So, you've had no contact with Jo Royle since then?" Meera asked.

"It's Jo Pierce now, remember?" Cheryl replied.

"Yeah," the detective sighed. So much had happened since the murder, despite the lack of any real progress in its investigation.

"A whole new family dynamic to deal with," Cheryl continued. "Husband Eddie and four-month-old baby. But, no, she's not returned any of my calls or emails. And, as far as I know, not accessed any of the services I referred her to."

"Not exactly a surprise."

"No."

"So look, unless she actually requests anything from Family Liaison," Meera went on, "I think it's best for me to just go through where we're at with the investigation and why it's being cold-cased."

After twelve months, the murder investigation team had learnt very little about the fatal stabbing of Lee Royle. There was no clear forensic or CCTV evidence. Plenty of motive for his killing, but all the known suspects had watertight alibis. And the theory that this might have been a professional hit became more and more implausible. To make something look as haphazard as this would require astonishingly intricate planning for it to work. So, though the case remained unsolved, the Senior Investigation Officer, Detective Chief Inspector Creighton was sticking to the hypothesis of a road rage attack by an assailant most probably unknown to the victim.

"Jo might not have wanted to keep in touch with the inquiry," Meera observed, "but we're duty-bound to keep her informed and let her know why we're winding it down."

"Yeah. But aren't we forgetting somebody here?"

"Who?"

"Him. The new husband. He's part of the family now. He might have a few questions."

"Yeah," Meera agreed. "When did he turn up, by the way?"

"Wasn't on our radar till well after Royle's funeral. Bit of a whirlwind romance, it seems. I did a background check. Bit of juvenile form, but nothing connected to this case."

"Hmm. Maybe we should have dug a little deeper."

"We were kind of busy with the Leyton Cross shootings by then. But I did find out a few things."

"Like what?"

"A very impressive business profile."

"Tell me," Meera insisted.

She nodded thoughtfully as Cheryl went through some details. Meera was now curious to meet the mysterious new character in this story. And as they pulled up in front of the mansion, there he was. Framed by the columns at the front entrance, looking proprietorial in jeans and an open-necked shirt.

"Random?" Eddie Pierce exclaimed. "What do you mean, random?"

Meera wished that she had chosen her words more carefully.

"What I meant to say," she backtracked, "is that attacks like this, that happen on the spur of the moment, as it were...well, they're often hard to follow up without any supporting evidence. They can often be the hardest murders to solve."

"Random," Eddie repeated under his breath, muttering the word indignantly. "And what about this eyewitness?"

"That was never properly verified. Just an anonymous phone call early in the investigation."

"And you didn't manage to trace it?"

"I'm afraid not, no."

"Great."

They had been shown through to a lavish reception room, and Meera had outlined the status of the Royle investigation as Eddie became increasingly agitated. Jo was much more calm. In fact, she looked serene, nestled in the large, cream, suede sofa, cradling a sleeping baby in her arms.

"So, what, is the case closed now?" she asked softly.

"A murder inquiry is never closed. It's just being wound down. And until there are any new leads..."

"Like what?" Eddie interrupted her tersely.

"Like someone coming forward. It often happens in cases like this. Someone close to the perpetrator who knows something. Or the perpetrator themself. Someone who wants to clear their conscience."

"So," Eddie said, "now you're just going to wait until the murderer hands themself in. Is that it?"

Meera thought it best not to rise to this. She simply shrugged in what she hoped was a placatory manner.

"Look, we know what the police thought of Lee," Jo added. "We never expected that your lot would make much fuss over his killing."

"That was never an issue in the investigation, I can assure you."

"Yeah, right," Eddie retorted.

Meera stole a long glance at this intense young man with fiery green eyes. The budding entrepreneur who had risen seemingly without trace, Cheryl had told her. A director of a small start-up tech company, which had used accessibility technology to develop phone apps designed to aid the visually impaired. When this had been bought out, he set up his own IT corporation with Jo as his business partner. As a teenager, Eddie Pierce had served six months at Feltham Young Offenders Institute. Nothing spectacular – just some small-scale drug dealing and credit card fraud that might be written off as the folly of precocious youth. Indeed, he was very open and contrite about the misdemeanours of his past and had recently set up a charity to promote the rehabilitation of juvenile offenders.

Meera studied this successful businessman and respectable pillar of the community. Well on his way to finding a place on *The Sunday Times* Rich List, he just happened to be married to the widow of Kent's biggest gangster.

He caught her stare with a narrow frown.

"Is that it, then?" he demanded.

"Well," she began, but at that moment the baby woke up and started mewling.

"Hey," Eddie stood up and walked over to his wife and child.

"I think she's hungry," said Jo.

"Let me take her for a bit." Eddie reached out. "He-eey," he sing-songed to his daughter as he gathered her up. "Shush, yeah, come to Daddy."

He gently rocked the fractious child. Jo stood up and took the baby from him.

"So," she said. "Unless there's anything else important that you have to tell us..."

"Right." Meera nodded at Cheryl Symons and they both stood up as well.

She had hoped that she might get something from Jo. She remembered the woman's reaction when they had first told her of Lee Royle's death. Of how she'd laughed out loud. Maybe it had just been a nervous response. But then there was that comment Commander Ray Spinks had made: that they should put her under surveillance, as if she were a suspect or a person of interest, at least.

And she realised that she had misread Jo as being simply calm and relaxed. It was more like some sort of emotional exhaustion; she looked washed-out, as though she had been through some kind of trauma. And Eddie seemed to be acting strangely with her. Clearly protective, but wary as well.

"I think you can find your own way out," he told them.

As Meera passed him, he glared at her. She held his stare.

"Something still might come up," she handed him a card with her contact details.

"What's this?" he frowned.

"If you have any information you might want to pass on."

"Right," he sneered. "But you do know that this isn't good enough. Not good enough at all."

As they walked out to the car, Meera Hussain began to catalogue in her mind all the things she would have to do with the case now. All of the administrative procedure. Evidence logged, exhibits stored, documents filed. Everything put neatly in order so that it could go into cold storage like so many others like it. But now all her doubts about the case came back to her. Had they missed something? She remembered questioning Spinks's connection to Lee Royle, and how she had suspected that he might have compromised the investigation. Eddie Pierce's words gave voice to her disquiet. Maybe he was right. That it was not good enough. Not good enough at all.

2

"They had a nerve," Eddie said to Jo once they had left. "Coming today of all days."

"Yeah," she sighed. "But now maybe we can put it all behind us."

"What?"

"You know, Lee's murder."

Eddie frowned at her. He was about to say something when the gate buzzer went. It was Craig, Jo's brother. He pulled up at the house in his black BMW 6-Series convertible. He had a present for the couple.

"Happy anniversary!" he declared as he proudly placed a bottle of Cristal champagne on the kitchen work surface.

They told him about the visit from the Kent Police.

"Out of order, them turning up like that," he commented. "Probably did it on purpose. You know what they're like."

"But what do you think?" Eddie asked him.

"They don't care. Lee killed a cozzer, and that was always going to count against him."

"That's what I said," Jo agreed.

"And, well," Craig shrugged. "Maybe they're right."

"What?" Eddie scowled.

"Maybe it was this road rage thing."

"What makes you say that?" Eddie snapped. "What the fuck do you know about it?"

There was an awkward silence for a moment as Eddie stared at his brother-in-law. Craig had never quite got over the sharp change in the power dynamic of their relationship, but he knew from experience that it was always best to placate his new boss. Jo looked on awkwardly, keenly feeling the buzz of aggression between the two men in her life.

"So" – Craig finally broke the tension with a broad grin – "where's Annie? Where's my favourite niece?"

Jo watched her brother pick up the baby. She smiled as little Annie gurgled with laughter at her uncle, then left them to it as she went to confront Eddie.

"What was all that about?" she demanded in a harsh whisper.

"Sorry, it's just this business with the investigation."

"Why are you getting so wound up about it?"

"They're not doing their job, Jo. Doesn't that bother you?"

"No," she shrugged. "Not really."

"What?"

"Look, Eddie, I'm just coming out of this fucking depression. I really don't need this. Not now."

"But…"

"And I don't care about Lee. I never did!" she snapped. "I never loved him the way I love you."

"Hey," Eddie said softly, but she had turned away from him.

"I'm going upstairs."

Later, as she stood before the bedroom mirror, getting ready to go out, she said to herself: *I'm not a bad person, really.*

It had been so hard after the birth of their child. Nightmares and panic attacks and long, bleak days full of self-loathing. She had been plunged into a paralysing sense of doom and guilt. The doctor had diagnosed postpartum depression. It was a common mood disorder, it was explained, often caused by hormonal changes and sleep deprivation. She was prescribed a course of anti-depressants, 100mg of Nortriptyline daily.

The drug numbed the pain and dulled her mind. But Jo knew that she was simply medicating herself so that she didn't have to face the true cause of her disturbed soul – something she could tell no one. The terrible secret that she had shared with Lee. The reason she had wished him dead.

Eddie had been at her side throughout all of this. That she could not tell him the truth added to her sickening sense of self-reproach. But she knew she had to keep this from him – for now, anyway. Otherwise, he might turn on her when she needed his trust most. He had made their home a sanctuary and made certain that she had everything she needed. He had got a live-in nanny, Gabriela from Romania, so that Jo could take time out when she needed to. Most of all, she wanted to be sure of him, even if she was uncertain of her own feelings.

But Eddie had his own dark places. The business they had founded was doing well, but she worried that power was making him paranoid. She was relieved that the investigation into Lee's death was being wound up, but it had stirred something up in Eddie. She didn't want any more digging around in her past. With the case closed, she could put it all behind her. But she knew now that she had to be certain. She had to take control of the situation, not allow herself to give in to remorse anymore. She had to be strong.

A gentle knock on the half-open door took her out of this reverie. It was Eddie.

"Are you decent?" he asked as he entered with a smile.

She turned to face him and then glanced back at her profile in the mirror.

"I could lose a few pounds," she sighed.

"No," he said flatly. "You look great."

Jo loved the fact that her new husband liked her with a fuller figure. Lee would have said something bitchy. Eddie came forward and one hand reached out to touch her lightly.

"Here," he said, holding something out to her.

It was a flat, oblong black box, with *Stephen Webster* embossed on it. Her favourite jeweller, who had done their wedding rings; a Kent native, like herself. She took it from him and opened the sprung lid.

"It's beautiful," she remarked softly.

It was a brooch in the form of the Eye of Horus, with a large sapphire as its centrepiece.

"It's meant to ward off evil," he told her.

"Yeah," she said, and at that moment all seemed well in their world.

But there was that frown again on Eddie's face.

"What?" she asked him.

"When I got the hump with Craig."

"Yeah?"

"Well, he was acting a bit weird."

"What do you mean?"

"About the murder inquiry."

"Was he?"

This was not how she had recalled it. It was Eddie that had been wound up over the whole thing.

"He wanted to change the subject all of a sudden."

"So?"

"I was with him on the day Lee was killed. He turned up late. And he was in a funny mood."

"Come on, you don't think he had anything to do with it?"

"I just don't buy this road rage angle, Jo. Too much of a fucking coincidence."

And, yes, she thought, he was right. It did seem like such a lucky accident. Some things were meant to be. But she didn't want Eddie to think about this too much. It was dangerous.

"What do you remember about that day?" she asked him, as if to deflect his curiosity.

"I don't know," he pressed the heel of his palm against his brow and let out a sharp breath. "It was the day I met you."

"Yeah," she frowned at him. "What's the matter?"

"Nothing. Just got a headache coming on." Eddie blinked and thought back to that fateful day. "I remember that morning. I'd been without a car for a couple of days, so I'd been spending too much time indoors. It was driving me crazy."

3

Craig had picked Eddie up outside his apartment block by the Thames in Greenhithe that Sunday. They were to collect Eddie's car from a garage in West Kingsdown where it was being fitted with a false compartment. The older man had noted the bleary look on his young apprentice.

"Rough night?" he gibed.

"I'm all right."

"You look wasted. Hope you're not getting high on your own supply."

"Course not. Cabin fever, that's all. Hope my motor's ready."

"It is."

"Good. Shouldn't we take a left here?"

"No, mate. We're going via Bluewater. There's a big snarl up on the M25."

For a moment, Eddie felt disorientated as they headed down the A206. He hated being a passenger; he always like to be in the driver's seat. And taking the London Orbital Motorway was second nature to him. It was where he learnt his trade.

He had started out working county lines, then, through hard graft, had worked his way up to be a top-level drug courier. Large-scale distribution became his business, running product around the M25. Wholesale quantities would be smuggled in through the Channel ports and loaded onto that great tarmac carousel to be trafficked inwards towards the city or outwards to the counties.

And that's where he had met Craig Cadmoor, one of the major dealers in Kent. Eddie was just the sort of ambitious, high-earning operator that got noticed as an asset to the syndicate. So he was recruited, with Craig as his direct boss and handler.

Eddie rubbed his face and let out a low groan.

"You really did have wild time, didn't you?" Craig chided him.

"Nah," Eddie shook his head slowly.

The fact was that he had been taking too much coke. And wasting his time playing computer games into the early hours. Burning away at boredom until his whole consciousness became a heightened virtual reality. There were flickering flashbacks of racing and combat.

"Well, pull yourself together," Craig went on. "You gotta be on your best behaviour today. We're going to make a stop on the way."

"What?"

"Lee wants to meet you."

Eddie had long known about this mysterious figure that was behind so much of the organised crime in the county. He'd first heard of him in Feltham. One of those legends that those doing juvenile time get obsessed with. The cop killer who had got off with a self-defence plea. Rumoured to be the man behind the Tunbridge Wells Cash Depot Job. A ruthless bastard who had got away with it all somehow. Just the sort of negative role model all the screws and the do-gooders that came and went seemed determined to steer all those aspiring young villains away from. But he was something of an ideal for Eddie. A gangster that had transformed himself into a successful businessman – an economic model he was determined to pursue himself. Craig clocked the wide-eyed look on his young subordinate's face.

"Well, that woke you up, didn't it?" he said. "So look lively. Make sure you don't do anything disrespectful in his presence. And watch your mouth. None of your clever talk."

"What do you mean?"

"You know what I mean. All that clever-school bollocks of yours. I might let you get away with it sometimes. Lee ain't so forgiving."

Craig glanced over to catch Eddie's broad grin.

"Don't get so excited. He just wants to check you out. And be careful. He might be measuring you up for something."

"What?"

Craig let out a long sigh.

"Look, he said. "The way it works is this: Lee is risk averse. Absolutely. He likes to think of himself as a lucky man, but what he really wants is others to be unlucky. You get me?"

"Explain."

"He always makes sure that others take the risk for him. And sometimes" – Craig shrugged – "sometimes they have to take the fall. So keep on your toes with Lee Royle."

"Right."

"He's been in this game a fucking long time, and to survive, he's had to be ruthless. He knows there's always a steady supply of young faces wanting to get into trouble for him."

"Like with the Tunbridge Wells Job?"

Craig turned to give Eddie a fierce glare.

"Well, for one thing, make fucking sure you don't mention that."

"I got you. Don't worry. I'll be the soul of discretion."

"Yeah. Whatever that means. Just don't push your luck."

"Right. Or let Lee Royle push it for me."

Craig laughed.

"Yeah," he said. "That's Lee's M.O., all right. He's been pushing other people's luck all his life. But one of these days, it might just push back at him."

"It's like he knew something was going to happen," Eddie said to Jo as she continued to dress.

"Yeah, well, it already had, hadn't it?"

"What?"

"Lee had already been murdered by then."

"And Craig was late picking me up that day."

"Wait a minute, I think we agreed long ago that Craig wouldn't have the bottle to do something like that. He's a follower, not a leader. Always has been."

"All those years of resentment? Of being in someone else's shadow? Think about it."

"I just don't see it. Now, come and zip me up."

As he came behind her, she caught his puzzled face in the mirror. Why was he getting so obsessed by this, just when it was all being put to rest. This could really fuck things up for her.

"You remember how Craig was that day?" he asked her.

"Not really," she said. "I remember you, though."

4

Jo had been preparing a leg of lamb. She remembered looking wistfully at the paring knife in her hand when she heard the front gates open. Lee had become so bloody predictable, she thought. Back from some Essex whore just in time for Sunday lunch. She sighed and continued to stab at the joint, studding it with cloves of garlic and sprigs of rosemary. As she caught the pungent scent of blood and herb, she listened for the dry static of tyre on gravel. Jocasta measured twenty years of betrayal and regret as she waited on her husband's slow and remorseless tread back to his lair.

They'd had a row the night before, over money. They had been feeling the pinch lately and Jo wanted some financial security. She had seen what often happened to villain's wives. Even those that were married to the clever ones, like Lee.

"You're set up in perpetuity," he had insisted. "There's money in the offshore accounts."

"Which I don't have any access to."

"You'll get that when the time comes. Not now. It's for your own benefit. So you're not an accessory if there's an investigation."

"But what about now?"

"Now?" he had replied, his face darkening with rage. "Now? You're a greedy bitch, you know that? I give you all of this and spend all week trying to get more, and when I come home, I get this. Well, fuck that! I'm going somewhere I'm appreciated."

As he stormed out, Jo thought, and not for the first time, that her husband was worth more to her dead than alive. Greedily sitting on that fortune he had carved up with Ray Spinks. It brought to mind that nursery rhyme: *the king was in his counting house, counting out his money.* That was Lee, for sure. If she could only find a way to fix that, she mused, as she heard him drive off into the night.

She finished dressing the meat and turned on the oven. She washed her hands and walked across the large open-plan kitchen to the window. Love had made her bitter. She had wasted her best years on him with little to show for it. Nothing had really moved on in her life. She was still that seventeen-year-old girl he had eyed up on the dancefloor at Flick's nightclub in Dartford.

And Lee had been so impressive back then. Still in his thirties, handsome and self-assured in an open-necked shirt and seersucker suit. One of her girlfriends went all wide-eyed when it was clear he was looking their way. *That's Lee Royle,* she had whispered sharply to Jo. He had a reputation in their part of the world. He was a face. Even Craig was intimidated by him, and he was one of the hardest kids in Bexleyheath. He called Lee Royle the "King of Kent" and was only half-joking.

Jo watched for his car to clear the trees that hid Sevengates from the road. But the vehicle that emerged wasn't Lee's Land Rover, but Craig's BMW. What did her brother want on a Sunday? she wondered. As the car braked by the fountain in front of the house, she went out to greet him.

"Lee about?" Craig called to her as he climbed out of the motor.

"Don't know where he is," she replied flatly.

As her brother loped across the gravel towards the front door, she saw someone get out of the passenger side. A young man who moved so much more pleasingly, with a fluid, animal grace. Craig pulled out his mobile and made a call. He frowned.

"Gone to voicemail," he said and ended the call.

"Aren't you going to leave a message?"

"I'll text him. No one listens to their voicemails anymore."

As Craig started to clumsily tap away at his device, Jo looked beyond, towards her brother's companion. A tautly muscled frame, rigged in jeans and tight pink polo shirt. A mop of auburn hair, cropped at the sides, framed a pale countenance and flinty green eyes. He had a slightly broken nose, lightly smattered with freckles. An imperfection that heightened the beauty of his face rather than marred it. Cherubic lips pouted mischievously.

His eyes flared a little as they turned on her. And at once, she was utterly disarmed by the way he looked at her. Not that leering, resentful gaze she got from men at her gym. This was more like an expression of wonder. A sort of lustful innocence. How old was this kid, early twenties? She smiled and let him take her in. His handsome face open, beatific.

It let her realise that she did look good, though she'd scarcely felt that way in a long time. Her blonde hair was tied back in a low chignon, bringing out the curves of her cheeks and the line of her jaw. Jo rested one hand on her hip, all at once confident in her body and the work she had done. Pilates, kickboxing, Ashtanga: all wasted on Lee. A physical rigour she had taken on that had almost become a substitute for sex. It maintained an impressive figure that filled out a cropped Puma sweatshirt and skin-tight Lululemon yoga leggings.

Craig looked up from his phone and caught her staring, following her gaze to the young man who now stood behind him.

"Thought I told you to wait in the car," he snarled.

"Oh, don't be like that, Craig," she said gently, knowing that her brother could be a soft touch. "Come in and have a drink. You, too."

She turned and smiled at Eddie as Craig sighed and walked past her towards the front door.

"Hi," she said. "I'm Jo."

"Eddie," he replied as she led him into the house and through to the kitchen.

She put the lamb in the oven and set the timer. Then she walked over to the fridge.

"Right, it's gone twelve," she declared. "Let's have a glass of wine."

Craig smirked as she pulled out a bottle of Beaujolais.

"Aw, sis," he chided her. "You're not supposed to keep red wine in the fridge."

"Actually," Eddie cut in, coming forward to gently take the bottle from Jo and study the label. "With a light-bodied red like this, that's precisely what you should do."

"See?" Jo added.

"I knew I should have made you wait in the fucking car," Craig snapped. "That mouth of yours is going to get you into so much trouble one day."

Jo laughed.

"Where did you find this one?" she demanded.

"This posh wanker? He's a middle-class dropout. Did A-levels and everything."

"Never finished, though," Eddie muttered.

"What, so no college? Or uni?" she asked him.

"Just Feltham Young Offenders Institution," he told her with a sad smile.

A good boy gone bad, she thought wistfully, with a displaced sense of yearning. For her own wasted years, and something else inside she still couldn't face about herself. Eddie had the charisma of a dark angel, or bright demon, already working the upper hand on Craig without him fully knowing that this apprentice was clearly intent on becoming master. He had learnt to be tough, with all the cockiness of youth and a ruthless sense of entitlement that came with his class.

But this lost soul would not find it so easy with Lee, she feared. He was just the sort of game young chancer that her husband liked to use up and eventually discard. Like poor, sad Chris Ipsworth. Young Eddie would have to watch himself there.

She poured the wine, and as they chinked, they made eye contact once more. An intimate, sacramental moment of connection. Jo suddenly felt that she knew Eddie on some deep level, like some memory. Just her mind playing tricks, of course. She didn't know him from Adam.

And as Craig started to make small talk, she turned away and nodded along to his chatter so that her brother would not suspect anything, just stealing the odd glance across the kitchen's central island. Eddie, too, made sure that his attention seemed focussed on the older man, only allowing his eyes to flicker in her direction intermittently. Odd flashes of communication between them that would remain encrypted, even to themselves. That shared puzzle of sudden attraction.

Eventually, Craig looked at his watch.

"Look, we better get on," he said, draining the rest of his wine. "See you later, sis."

He stood up, kissed her on the cheek and turned back to Eddie.

"Doesn't look like you're going to meet the boss today, after all."

"Right," said Eddie, and stood up to leave.

"See you again," Jo said, struggling to make it sound off-hand, casual.

"Yeah," he promised quietly, and followed Craig out to the car.

5

"You had a lot of front," Jo said as they drove to the restaurant. "Looking at me like that."

"Well, you looked back."

"I did."

"What were you thinking?"

"Honestly?"

"Yeah."

"I looked at you and thought: I wish my husband was dead."

They laughed.

"And then he was," said Eddie.

"Yeah."

"Love is ruthless."

His voice was cold all of a sudden. She looked over at him.

"What do you mean?" she asked.

"I mean it gets what it wants. Like fate."

"Don't start that."

"What?"

"All that destiny stuff. Like we don't have a say in it. I chose you, Eddie. I wanted you, and I got you."

"You certainly did," he smiled.

"And, what? You just went along with it? With this 'fate' of yours?"

"Of course not. I'm just saying that from the first moment I saw you, I knew it was meant to be."

"Yeah?"

"Yeah," he insisted, to himself as much as to her. "Me and you. It had to be. I didn't know where I was until I saw you. Who I was, even. Meeting you, well, it gave my life meaning."

She laughed gently but he knew it was true. He had known it back then.

They had left Sevengates, and he had picked up his newly customised Jeep Cherokee from the garage in West Kingsdown. He was back behind the wheel again. Driving had always given him a sense of purpose, though it was the love of it that had got him into trouble in the first place. He had barely passed puberty when he was hotwiring motors and joyriding around his quiet neighbourhood.

Eddie Pierce had been born in greenbelt suburbia. The precious only child of a respectable, middle-class couple. But he had always felt bad, out of place amid his gentile upbringing. As long as he could remember, lies and deceit had come second nature to him. And he seemed compelled to enact casual acts of cruelty even as a boy.

His parents were convinced that he would grow out of this disturbing behaviour, but as he reached adolescence, the nature of his misdemeanours became ever more illicit. His teachers were baffled. He was clearly an intelligent boy – sensitive, even. He simply didn't seem to be able to make any agreement with the ordinary, decent life that should have been his. He rejected every option except that which was forbidden. It was discovered that he had been dealing drugs in school. He defrauded his father's credit card. He stole a car and drove halfway across the country until he was arrested and brought back to face judgment.

Six months in Feltham completed his unsentimental education. Any notion that this harsh regimen might intimidate him into goodness was soon dashed, as he displayed a seemingly innate aptitude for ruthlessness towards his fellow inmates. He was picked on at first, but he soon learnt how to fight back. He developed quick responses and hardened himself with a vicious streak so that the bullies backed off, leaving him free to absorb the culture of his new environment in a thoroughly diligent study of vice.

His parents forgave him and begged for his return on his release date. He knew that they had only ever tried their best for him, but he despised them thoroughly for that. They had tried to smother him, and thoughts of their dull and comfortable life filled him with a murderous rage. He felt dispossessed. Alone. He knew that he could never go back.

Instead, he found a new vocation, orbiting that very suburban interzone that had tried so hard to nurture him into a straight life. Distribution became his trade, running drugs around the M25 circular motorway. Eddie would pick-up and drop-off at lorry parks, service stations, Travelodge hotels. He would find himself doing deals in sleepy satellite towns, all identical to the one he had grown up in. This was his domain: subtopia. A labyrinth of retail parks and industrial estates; reservoirs and golf courses; film studios and abandoned mental asylums. A manicured landscape picked out by electricity pylons and Victorian water towers, reservoirs and flooded gravel pits.

He seemed happiest when on the move, as if speed could give him the escape velocity needed to defy the enervating gravity of these banal edgelands. But each acceleration merely took him closer to his starting point. He felt trapped in a decaying orbit, in a continuous, endless fall.

He even tried the drugs he dealt in the hope of achieving some mind-altered state. But they just sped things up or slowed things down. In his waking hours, he was driven by some unspoken fate. And even his dreams were repetitive, circular. Functional without meaning. He had visions of death, or sex, the only realities that seemed to offer a way out.

So he sought bodily release through mobile dating sites and hook-up apps, scanning profiles that offered some seductive simulacrum of humanity. He created avatars of his own which seemed, even to himself, more convincing than his own hollow being. Sexual transactions were negotiated in a perfunctory manner, as easy as his drug deals. He soon realised that both were a simple matter of supply and demand, a polymorphous exchange of bodies, body parts, body fluids. He joined all sorts of networks: straight, gay, bi, and trans. He became ever more curious of dark sites that linked violence with sexuality. But the emptiness inside just got deeper and wider. He met a woman in Slough who liked to pretend she was dead as they copulated. One Monday morning, he found himself in a room in Fulham full of naked men, fucking and sucking each other, as they gazed at high-definition porn on a huge flatscreen. All utterly deranged on GHB, mephedrone, and crystal methamphetamine.

He felt an appalling loneliness and yearned for that one true contact that might save him. Round and round he had gone, riding the snake that devours its own tail.

But he now felt powered by a new energy. A true desire. That moment with Jo Royle had given him some sense of purpose. He didn't know what it meant yet, but he somehow knew that it would break him from the loop that his life seemed trapped in.

He passed a brownfield site, the levelled ruins of a light industrial complex. A precinct of decayed concrete grouted with moss; a warehouse skeleton choked with weeds. The wild was taking it back, mother nature reclaiming her bastard countryside. Eddie wondered how many orbits it would take before it was all overgrown. And he was suddenly hungry for a new life that might now be his.

A curious sense of certainty possessed him at that moment. Driving was prophecy, he felt sure of it, accelerating him towards his destiny. The highway, with its signs and markings, was leading him to where he was meant to be.

And now, over a year later, he was determined not to lose that feeling of determination. Everything else had fallen into place. He had got all that he had wanted. There was just one missing piece in the puzzle: Who had killed Lee Royle?

And it seemed to threaten his very integrity. Unless this could be resolved, he felt that he might be thrown back into the chaos of his past. He needed certainty and could not afford any doubt in his world.

"The thing is," he told Jo over dinner. "We know what happened with all the rest. But this is just…"

He shrugged.

"What?" Jo demanded.

"Hanging over us."

"Maybe we should just leave it like that."

Eddie felt a surge of rage rise up in him.

"Why am I the only person who seems to be bothered about this?" he seethed. "The police don't want to know. Craig goes along with this road rage thing. And you?"

"Look–"

"He was your husband, Jo. Doesn't that count for anything?"

"But don't you see? They're winding up the investigation, that means they're not snooping around us. That's got to be a good thing."

"Maybe."

As he looked out into the middle distance, she tried to catch his eye. She hoped at that moment that he might drop the whole thing.

"But he's still out there, isn't he?"

"What? Who?"

"The killer."

"Oh. Yeah, I suppose so."

"Well, that's not a risk I'm prepared to take. And not with you or with my daughter."

"Oh, come on, Eddie."

"I mean it, Jo. If this guy isn't caught, it could destroy us."

"You really think so?"

Eddie was now so wound up that Jo didn't want to contradict him anymore.

"Fuck the police," he went on. "We can do a better job than they did."

"What? What do you mean?"

"I'm going to find out who killed Lee: that's what I mean."

There seemed nothing she could do to dissuade him from this course of action, and she knew it would mean trouble. So she tried to unravel all the events that had led up to this moment, to work out what Eddie knew or did not know about her past. She remembered the day she had first learnt of Lee's death.

6

When the police had arrived at Sevengates on that Monday morning, Jo assumed that Lee had been arrested the day before. This was why he hadn't turned up or replied to Craig's message. That he'd not made any attempt to contact her in the meantime didn't surprise her either, since she knew he wasn't likely to waste his mandatory phone call on her if he had been taken into custody. He'd have called his lawyer, Brian Colby, first. Lee would have taken it for granted that Jo would know what to do when the cozzers came calling. She buzzed them through the gate and went outside to wait for them.

It was then she began to sense that something unforeseen had occurred. She had expected the Heavy Mob. The Serious Crime Squad, team-handed and tooled up, with a brief to turn the house upside-down. What she saw was a small, unmarked car with two plainclothes women officers in it.

It pulled up in the drive and they both got out and approached her.

"I'm Cheryl Symons," announced one, showing her ID. "Family Liaison Officer with Kent Police. This is Detective Constable Hussain. Can we have a word?"

"You're not coming in here without a warrant," Jo insisted.

"We're not here to make a search, Mrs Royle," Detective Constable Hussain explained. "I'm afraid we've got some bad news."

"Oh," Jo gasped, looking at each sombre face in turn. "We better go inside, then."

She led them into the house, and they sat at the dining room table as Cheryl Symons slowly went through what had happened. Jo tried to concentrate but felt herself drifting off. None of it seemed real.

She tried to listen intently to what was being said, but it seemed absurd. The concerned tone didn't help – a soft voice that became a meaningless drone. Kindness and sympathy from the police? They started to detail organisations that could offer emotional support or practical advice. For what? It didn't make any sense.

Then Detective Constable Hussain intervened with a sharper tone. When had she last had contact with her husband? That was more like it. Questions she could answer or give no comment to. But then there was a look between the two women. A sense that any kind of tangible interrogation was inappropriate at this time.

Cheryl Simmons started talking again and, conscious of the look of confusion on Jo's face, gently reiterated what they had come to tell her. As it slowly sank in, Jo struggled to comprehend the news.

That Lee was dead.

She laughed out loud, then swiftly covered her mouth, her eyes wide with embarrassed consternation.

"Sorry," she said. "It's just the shock of it."

"Of course," Cheryl Symons rejoined with a sympathetic smile.

But Meera Hussain looked at her with a sharper intent, as if peering into her soul.

Shit, Jo thought. They know. It was as if they could detect her guilt, that she had wanted her husband dead. She had to remind herself that there was nothing anybody could pin on her. She had simply wished it. Somebody else had done the job for her. But maybe they were trying to catch her out. She looked at each woman in turn and nodded when she was asked if she was prepared to view the body. To confirm the identity. Yes, she would do that. It would keep her mind clear, her responses cold.

So she went with them in the car to the mortuary. As she was shown through to a tiled room with fluorescent lighting, she was warned to prepare herself.

And there he was, on the slab. This was the truth of the matter, the hard evidence of what they had told her. Corporeal. The deceased. A grievous word made dead flesh. *Oh, Lee*, her mind chided him, *what have you gone and done now?* Then she reasoned that he'd never have to worry about the consequences of his actions ever again. He was out of trouble for good.

And it struck her what a good corpse he made, like he'd finally relaxed. Looking supremely serene, lying in state as it were, his marbled flesh sculptured, imperious. The eyes were closed, the brow slightly furrowed in a noble frown, as if puzzled by his fate. His lips flattened in a pout of disdain, an expression that suited his readiness for oblivion. For a moment, Jo imagined that some trace of cognition yet dwelt on this face. But no, thought was elsewhere. Life was elsewhere, she realised.

Lee Royle was dead. And here was the proof of it. The ruins of a formidable man. Jo suddenly wanted to say something, to tell him that she wished that it could have been better between them, to claim all that love she had wasted on him. But it was too late for that now.

He had got what he deserved; that was the truth of the matter. She knew that she didn't have to feel guilty for anything, even though she still blamed herself for what had happened. And she knew that she would have to give the world some appearance of grief. But as she took one last look at him, she struggled to find any words or even thoughts of lamentation. Her mind seemed empty, her feelings numb. He was just a man, after all. She turned from the body to face the others in the room.

"Yeah," she told them. "That's him."

The day had become hot as they drove back to Sevengates. Heavy clouds brooded on the horizon. The sky was charging up as they arrived at the house.

Cheryl Symons went through some last details of her role and gave Jo an information booklet, urging her to contact various agencies and services. Jo promised she would, if only to placate the worried look on this woman's face.

Then, Detective Constable Hussain came forward.

"I'm your Case Worker on this investigation," she said in a colder, more detached tone. "I'm your contact with regards to anything pertaining to the investigation itself."

Jo recognised the professional gaze that met hers. *This one's a real cozzer,* she thought. *I better watch this one.*

"We'll want a statement from you, in due course," the DC went on. "You might want a solicitor present."

"Yeah, I might."

"And we want to keep this quiet until the press conference on Wednesday, if that's all right with you. As you can imagine, there's going to be a bit of a media scrum over this."

"Yeah."

"If you want to be present, let us know."

Detective Constable Hussain handed her a card with her details and direct number.

"I've got nothing to say to that scum," Jo replied.

Hussain's phone rang.

"Sorry," she said. "I've got to take this."

Jo watched carefully as the detective turned away from her to answer the call.

"Yes, sir… Yes, we're done here. What, now? This afternoon?" she sighed. "OK. I'll need to drop Cheryl off first, though."

Cheryl Symons looked over and frowned at her colleague as she ended the call.

"Got to go to the Yard," Hussain explained. "Speak to someone there. Come on."

As she watched them get back into the car, Jo wondered what all that was about. She knew that Lee's death would have repercussions throughout the police service, including the Met.

The air was close as they drove away. The sun raged amid dark clouds in gold and purple. Jo felt an oppressive intimacy in the atmosphere. A storm was coming.

And Jo had her own arrangements to make. She took out her phone and began to scroll down her contacts. So many things she needed to sort out. She should talk to their lawyer Brian Colby first, she thought. He would need to know all the details of the investigation. Then there was the funeral, of course. Lee would want something big and vulgar. A parade of black limousines and gaudy floral tributes. She would phone her brother Craig, she decided. He'd be able to coordinate all these things. She scrolled some more, wondering what she would say to Craig. She knew what he would say: *the King of Kent is dead, who's going to take over now?* A bitter smile played on her lips.

This was the reality she had to deal with now. She had to take control, and at that moment she wished that she had somebody in her corner, watching her back. Craig and Brian Colby had their own agendas; she couldn't trust them entirely. She needed someone else close, someone just working for her.

7

Commander Ray Spinks sat in his office on the fifth floor of New Scotland Yard and glared at the report that had come thudding back onto his desk once more. The four hundred and fifty-three pages of managerial gobbledegook provisionally titled: *Contracting Out Services in the Metropolitan Police Service and its impact on Specialist Units*. Spinks had been working on this mind-numbingly dull work of literature for nearly four years.

And now it was being returned to him for the nineteenth time with a glossy bound document and a memo attached from the Deputy Assistant Commissioner. *Dear Ray, Note the new recommendations from City Hall. We'll need revisions on sections 3, 5, 6, 7 & 14 at the very least. Can you liaise with MOPAC on this? Best regards, Frank.* He unpicked the note from the document it was paperclipped to. A colour-coded thing from the London Assembly's Budget and Performance Committee called: *To Protect and Save: The Met's Approach to Outsourcing.* Spinks sighed with a deep dread. It was only Monday afternoon, and he already wanted to kill someone.

They were doing this to punish him, of course. He'd reasoned that long ago. This was their revenge. Revenge for all the failed investigations he'd been subject to; the inconclusive reports on police corruption that mentioned him; the unproven complaints of procedural misconduct. Revenge for all the Form 163's that had been served on him in the course of his career, informing him of allegations made that he had breached the standards of professional behaviour.

Because none of it had stuck. Nothing had been proved. There was not a speck of dirt on his police record. No one had ever got to the truth of the matter. He remained inscrutable, an enigma. He had a genius for being cryptic, right back to when he had first worked as a detective and had a fondness for using obscure conundrums while interrogating suspects to throw them off guard.

He had once been brilliant, a consummate thief-taker in the making. But he'd been too keen, too ambitious to get results and get ahead. And he'd found out far too easily that the best way to get information was to play the game both ways. That the best way to understand the criminal mind was to think and act like one. It was a heady game that soon became all too real. And his success rate became intoxicating. He found that he could use his considerable investigative talents to put enough villains away to advance his career, all whilst lining his own pockets. And he had hidden his trail as only a great detective could.

There were always suspicions, of course. But no one could quite solve the riddle that was Ray Spinks, a name that had come up in so many anti-corruption operations only to be cleared of any wrongdoing. There had been a consistent failure in any attempt to bring him to book, dismiss, or even discipline him. It was then seen as expedient that he should retire. To make a quiet exit, to disappear discreetly. To go away and sin no more. But he wouldn't give them that satisfaction. That would only seem to confirm his guilt. It would be an admission of defeat. Oh, no, he was going to serve out his term.

So they tortured him with this huge and meaningless report. The punishment should fit the crime, after all. Let him riddle his way out of this one, seemed their taunt to his cleverness. And they trapped him in a maze of paperwork.

So he felt some sense of reprieve when reception called and told him that a Detective Constable Meera Hussain from Kent Police wanted to see him.

"Send her up," he told them.

Meera Hussain had short, dark hair and wore a dark-blue skirt suit. Ray Spinks nodded at the chair opposite him.

"Take a seat, Constable," he said. "What can I do for you?"

"I'm part of a team investigating an incident by Junction 1A of the M25 yesterday."

"Oh, yeah? What is it?"

"A fatal stabbing, sir."

"Right."

"We've ID'd the victim, but we don't want to release the name just yet."

"Why not?"

"Well," she shrugged, "we want to be ready for the press. They're going to go mad on this one. We want to get all the intelligence we can on the victim before that."

"What about next of kin?"

"Me and Family Liaison saw his wife this morning."

Spinks frowned.

"Then you came straight here to see me?"

"Yes. My guvnor thinks that your, um, specialised knowledge of the victim could be crucial to the investigation."

Spinks smiled and looked straight at her.

"All right," he shrugged. "I give up. Who is it?"

"It's Lee Royle, sir."

He didn't even blink. He even allowed himself a short laugh as he kept his stare fixed on hers.

"Haven't heard that name in a while."

"He was your informant, sir."

"That was a long time ago, Detective Constable. So, who killed him?"

"Haven't even got a clear suspect yet, sir."

"Well, plenty of people wanted him dead," he smiled once more. "Some of them in the Job."

"Yes, well…"

"Listen," Spinks narrowed his gaze on her. "A lot has been made of my, er, association with Lee Royle. But that was long before the Tunbridge Wells business or that operational cock-up that led to an undercover surveillance officer getting killed."

"I'm sorry sir, but Detective Chief Inspector Creighton wanted a full background profile on the victim and pointed me in your direction."

"What? George Creighton?"

"Yes, sir. He's the Senior Investigation Officer on this one."

"Right."

Good old George, thought Spinks. *One of the old firm. Giving me the heads up before all the dogs are out of their traps.* He nodded slowly at Detective Constable Meera Hussain.

"You should have said," his voice softened and became wistful. "Me and George worked Regional Crime Squad together back in the 1980s. That's when Lee Royle was my snout. Feeding me knowledge about lorry hijacks on the A2. And making a fair amount out of reward money and payments from the Information Fund from it. I moved on in the Met and lost touch with him. Then our names get put together after the Tunbridge Wells thing. But remember, he was never convicted of being part of the robbery or the conspiracy. Only as an accessory after the fact, and at that, a very minor one. And I knew nothing about any of it. He stuck up my name after he was arrested for killing that undercover officer SO11 put in his garden one night. Royle was trying to do some sort of deal, I imagine. But he didn't have to. No, that operation was so cack-handed. I mean, send in a guy to do surveillance in camouflage and a fucking balaclava? At night in his fucking garden? No wonder Royle got off with a self-defence plea. He just had to claim he thought the guy was a hitman."

"But Royle did go away for the Tunbridge Job."

"As I said, as an accessory. Did five years of a seven stretch."

"Some of the money from the robbery was never recovered."

"No," Royle sighed. "And that's one of the mysteries of our time."

"Yes, I suppose it is, sir."

"What are your initial leads on the investigation?"

"From what we've got so far, it looks like a random assault. Road rage, perhaps."

"Really?"

"Though it could be a very well organised hit made to look like that. We're trying to narrow down every line of enquiry. And, as I said, we want to be ahead of the press on this. That's why we want to gather as much information as we can on Royle and of all his known associates. So if anything comes to mind, sir…"

"Well, Chris Ipsworth is just out of prison. Lead robber on the Tunbridge Wells Job. He's bound to be a person of interest."

"He's certainly on our radar, sir. Still a very dangerous individual."

"Well, let's keep in touch on this one. You say you saw the wife today?"

"Yes, sir."

"You want to watch out for that one. Jo Royle, she's a clever bitch. Might be worth doing a covert on her."

"I'll bear that in mind, sir."

"And give George my regards, won't you? Tell him I owe him lunch."

George would know what that meant, thought Spinks as he stood up to show Detective Constable Meera Hussain to the door. Now he had to move fast. Lee Royle was dead. And there was someone he had to see.

8

Terry Rice sat at an outside table of Maison Bertaux patisserie on Greek Street. Feeling at home at this end of Soho, where one could get one's bearings from this archaic thoroughfare. It was the acoustics more than anything else, the rough music of the street with all its songs of gossip that reverberated down the years: Oscar Wilde feasting with panthers at Kettners, Thomas De Quincey eating opium in the garret of number 58, Giacomo Casanova taking lodgings at number 47 so he could be close to a French courtesan in St Giles. And resonance of more recent scandal: from the dive bars and the clip joints, the walk-up flats where working girls traded flesh, and dismal pubs where hacks bartered stories. Nearly all gone now, Terry mused, though the echoes still rang out. Perhaps one could catch a whisper of something coming out of Soho House, the private members club for media types across the road from the patisserie, but it wasn't quite the same. Despite that, Greek Street remained for Terry an auditorium of ancient rumour: classical, mythological.

Because it had always been Terry's vocation to listen, to tune in to the detail of something amid a cacophony of information, from an early age learning how to eavesdrop and, through that, to develop considerable investigative skills. Not so much a private eye but a private ear. Lacking one sense that enhanced all the others, possessed of an impairment that endowed another peculiar advantage for their chosen tradecraft. An ability to go about unsuspected, unnoticed even. They had found out long ago that being blind could also make you invisible.

Though, not for the kind staff at Maison Bertaux. A waiter approached and began to place things on the table.

"Rum baba to your right, Terry. Lapsang souchong to your left."

"Thank you, Paul."

And though that commonly held notion that it enhanced the hearing was true enough, it was more than merely acute: it was psychic. An advanced technology of listening had endowed in Terry a second sight that could predict things. It was a practise that had once been defined as augury: a divination of knowledge from birds and their flight. A more modern tradecraft was found in channelling another power of the air, for Terry was one of the best phone hackers in the business. And through this skill, had learnt how to interpret the birdsong of humanity.

Terry had started young. A lonely blind kid who found the telephone the most exciting thing in the world to play with. It kept little Terry company, its handset both toy and comfort, its dialling tone a soft and reassuring purr. They'd call up the speaking clock just to hear its soothing voice and to be connected to that safe, dark world where there was only sound. This was the land of the blind, where the blind from birth was king. And these were the happy, analogue days of rotary-dials, capacitors, and hookswitches. They soon discovered ways of fooling with the machine. Tapping out codes on the cradle or listening carefully for the exact tone that activated switchboards. They had perfect pitch and found that by whistling a seventh-octave E at 2600 Hertz the line would disconnect. The telephone exchange would think that they had hung up, but they were still inside the system, free to roam around it and make mischief. "Phone phreaking", it was called back then. In time, Terry found that there was a living to be made from this skill.

"Hello, Terry," came the sullen voice of Commander Ray Spinks.

"Ray. Such a pleasure not to see you. Have a seat."

Spinks sat and ordered a black coffee.

"What do you want, Ray?"

Spinks let out a singular laugh.

"Sorry," Terry went on. "You want some small talk first? How are you, Ray?"

"Fine. And you're looking well. A little on the butch side, if you don't mind me saying."

It was true. Terry was wearing a man's suit. The first time they had done that in decades.

"Well, there's news in that department. Later. Let's get to the point, shall we? What do you want?"

"I said on the phone, Terry. I've got something for you."

"*Quid pro quo*, Ray. That's what it means, if I know you. You want something. So, how many quid are we looking at?"

"For you, Terry, a few – quite a few. I nice little story you can sell to one of the red tops."

"And in return?"

"Oh, just a little bit of your magic."

It was an expertise in what became known as the "dark arts" that had put Terry at a nexus of illegal information trading. Hacking into voicemails or tracing someone's exact whereabouts; finding out secrets and mapping out profiles. It was in this arena that Terry had first come across Commander Spinks, who ran his own sideline in illicit data exchange. There'd been a boom time in demand for exposés on politicians, celebrities, even royalty. But it had all gone a bit too far, especially when it was discovered that a murdered girl's phone had been hacked by someone working for the press. An inquiry followed and a couple of scapegoats took the fall, but Terry had managed to stay under the radar.

"So what's the story?"

"Lee Royle."

"Ah, your old friend Lee. What's he done now?"

"Got himself killed."

"That's a bit careless. Who did it?"

"We don't know."

"Plenty of suspects. Chris Ipsworth's been out of jail for a while now. There's a man with motive for you."

"Yes, well…"

"Though, the funny thing is," Terry went on, "Lee always seemed to have some sort of hold over that man."

"Really?"

"Yes. Of course, the whole robbery was set up to fail so that certain parties would take the blame so that others could pocket their unfair share of the loot. Poor old Chris does eighteen years with less than nothing to show for it and yet he still shies away from going after Royle. Did he finally take his revenge?"

"Doesn't look like that, Terry. It looks like a random event. Road rage."

"Road rage?"

"Yeah, he got stabbed just off the M25 yesterday lunchtime. Looks like it started as an altercation."

"What a way to go."

"You appreciate the dramatic irony. So will the media, I'm sure. Thing is, the investigation team are withholding the identity of the victim in this case, so it's a chance to sell it to one of the tabloids quickly. Should be a splash. But make sure they get the road rage angle."

"For the dramatic irony?"

"You know, the killer who got away with it, brought down by their own fate. There's a sort of natural justice to it."

"Hmm. Sounds like you want to make sure the investigation's concluded rather quickly. What are you up to, Ray?"

"Never you mind."

"I mean, perhaps it's meant to look like road rage when in fact it's a very well-planned assassination."

"It would take a very good villain to pull that one off."

"Or an experienced police officer. Did you have him killed, Ray?"

"Don't be ridiculous."

"Well, you two do have something of a history."

"Look, I've got you a nice story to sell. Do you want it or not?"

"What do you want in return?"

"I want you to hack into Jo Royle's phone for me."

"You know the Royle syndicate uses an encrypted phone system?"

"That doesn't surprise me."

"They're like normal mobiles, but they've got a hidden app pre-installed. End-to-end secure with a remote-wipe feature."

"You mean you can't do it?"

"I didn't say that."

"I'm sure it's not beyond your considerable talents."

"No. But it's not easy. I want to make sure it's worth my while."

"Look, I'm giving you a big story. It's a splash. Front page. Could get you twenty grand, at least."

"Small change compared to what this information might be worth."

"Well, let's see, shall we? I'll come around to yours tomorrow and we can see what we've got, can't we?"

"Yeah."

"Don't get greedy, Terry."

"I just want what I'm due, that's all."

"Right," Spinks sighed. "I've things to do. Let me go through all the details of the Lee Royle story and you can get it placed somewhere before tonight's deadline."

9

COP KILLER ROYLE VICTIM OF ROAD RAGE MURDER screamed the headline in *The Sun* the following morning. Eddie picked up a copy at WH Smiths at South Mimms Services. He was there to meet a dealer called Jamal who ran county lines up through Hertfordshire. He scanned the front page as he walked across to Starbucks. *In an exclusive revelation* The Sun *can confirm that the victim of the M25 road rage killing was none other than Lee Royle, the notorious Kent crook and cop killer*…ran the standfirst. His contact was at a corner table. Eddie wandered over and dropped the newspaper in front of him.

"Fuck," Jamal gasped. "Your boss."

"Yeah," Eddie muttered as he sat down.

"What's going to happen now?"

"Fuck knows."

Eddie felt the phone in his pocket buzz. He pulled it out. There was a text from Craig. **Have U seen the news?**

Eddie quickly tapped a response. **Yeah.**

His mind was reeling, but as his thoughts settled on Jo, a faint smile played on his lips.

"Are you OK?" Jamal asked.

Eddie looked up, still distracted.

"What?"

"You look happy, bruv."

Eddie shook his head. But thinking of her filled him with such joyful anticipation. And with her husband dead, this could give him a chance.

"I get you," Jamal went on. "You see an opportunity in crisis."

Eddie laughed out loud at how close this young hustler from Tottenham was to reading his mind. Jamal joined in briefly, then looked stern for a second.

"Well, don't let your mind wander too far. Be careful," he warned Eddie. "Things could get heavy in Kent."

"Yeah. Maybe."

Jamal shrugged.

"Well, if you need to look after yourself. I could help you out."

"What do you mean?"

"When things get heavy, you might need to walk heavy."

"I don't think so."

"I could sort you out. I could get you something."

"Jamal…"

"I mean it. I could get you something sweet. A nice Glock 17."

As well as dealing drugs, Jamal had started a lucrative side-hustle of sourcing just the sort of merchandise needed in that profession. Firearms, untraceable vehicles, forged documents. He was a true entrepreneur.

"I'll let you know," Eddie said, and felt his phone buzz once more. He looked at the screen, it was Craig again. Come to Sevengates asap.

"I've got to go," he said and stood up.

"Aren't you forgetting something?" Jamal demanded,

pulling out a holdall from under the table. "Christ, your mind really is wondering."

"So, you've heard about Lee," Jo said.

She was on the phone to their lawyer, Brian Colby.

"There was something on the news this morning," he replied. "But it hasn't actually been confirmed yet."

"It was on the front page of *The Sun*."

"Yes. Not exactly the Newspaper of Record."

"Brian, I saw him. On the slab. Dead as a fucking dodo."

Colby sighed.

"I'm sorry, Jo. It's all just taking a while to sink in, that's all."

"Tell me about it."

"It must be awful for you. Look, I'm so sorry…"

"Can we keep this businesslike, Brian?" she cut in sharply.

"Sure."

"Something Lee might have left for me? With you?"

"Er…yeah. The paperwork, you mean?"

"I need it, Brian. And fast."

"It's in a safe deposit box. I can get it tomorrow. You could pick it up from my office?"

"I'd rather not come there, Brian. There might be prying eyes."

"Yes," he agreed. "Quite. Look, why don't you come to the house after work. Say, six o'clock?"

"I'll see you then," she said, and ended the call.

She walked through to the kitchen where Craig was sat nursing a cup of coffee. It worried her that her brother seemed more rattled by Lee's death than she was.

"I've spoken to Colby," she told him. "We'll soon know where we are money-wise."

"In the meantime, we need to let everybody know that we're still in control. That it's still business as usual. And if someone is trying to take over, well…"

"Take it easy, Craig. Lee just got into some stupid fight."

"We don't know that, yet. And Chris Ipsworth's just out of prison."

"Well, we'll know pretty soon if that one's making a move. Keep everybody else sweet, Craig. Let them know that there's plenty to go around, as always. And while you're doing that, I'll work things out with Brian."

The front gate buzzer went, and Jo went out to the hall.

"It's Eddie," came a voice from the speaker.

"What?"

"Craig told me to come over."

Jo buzzed him in and turned to her brother who had followed her out.

"Why's he coming here?"

"Just to be around. While I'm out."

"I can look after myself, Craig."

"Look, I just don't want to leave you on your own right now."

She nodded. She knew what this was all about. He wanted someone to keep an eye on her. Well, she would see about that.

10

"Call me straight away if anything comes up," Craig told Eddie as he prepared to leave. "Anything, right?"

"Look," Jo protested. "I really don't need this right now. I'm OK."

"Trust me, sis. We need to be careful. There are a lot of enemies out there that could take advantage of this. Some so-called friends, too."

"Well, aren't we're forgetting somebody here? Top of the fucking list."

Craig sighed.

"Spinks," he said.

"Yeah." Jo let out a hollow laugh and shook her head. "You don't even know where to start with that one, do you?"

"It was Lee's thing, you know that. He kept all that very close."

"And that's how he controlled you all. You fucking mugs. Now we don't know where we stand, do we?"

"Look, I'll be back soon. We can talk about it then," Craig said, and walked out to his car.

Jo sighed and turned to Eddie.

"Come on, then," she told him. "You want a cup of tea?"

In the kitchen, as she clicked on the kettle, she heard a dog whimper and scratch at the door to the back porch. It was Fraser, a six-year-old Doberman.

"Wait there," she told the young man. "I'm going to let him in. Careful, he can be a bit fierce."

Fraser gave out a little yelp, bounding into the space as she opened the door.

"Stay!" Jo ordered.

The dog froze and stared at the stranger. He let out a low growl.

"Come on, boy," Eddie entreated softly, and Fraser padded over to him.

Jo smiled as she watched her dog allow itself to be patted, panting enthusiastically as if it had caught the scent of something familiar.

"He's not like that with everyone," she said. "You must have some sort of gift."

"Yeah," he replied, pushing gently at the beast so that it curled up around his feet. "Look, I'm really sorry about your husband."

"I'm not," she shot back, coldly. "Sorry, does that shock you?"

Eddie shrugged.

"Maybe *you're* in shock," he offered.

"Maybe," she wondered, with the liberating feeling that she could be so frank and open with this near stranger. "But I don't think so."

He came closer.

"You must think I'm a heartless bitch," she said as the boiling water softly roared.

"I think you're beautiful," he told her.

She caught his stare, his flinty eyes fixed in a princely squint. His lips were open, expectant. His face seemed a mask of harsh desire.

Then the kettle clicked off and the tension broke for a moment.

"Fuck tea," she said breezily, walking towards a phalanx of bottles on the work surface. "I'm going to have a proper drink. You want one?"

"Why not?"

She picked up a bottle of Tanqueray and started to fix them two gin and tonics.

"Well, I'm the grieving widow," she announced. "I'm entitled."

She poured two large measures of spirit, added tonic and ice and lemon.

"So," she said, handing him a glass. "My brother wants you to look after me."

"I guess," Eddie grinned.

"Not the smartest one in the family, our Craig."

"Is that you, then?"

"I used to think so," Jo sighed. "And he wants you to spy on me?"

"He didn't say."

"But you work for him, right?"

"I wish I worked for you," he said softly, plaintively.

"Do you, now?"

"Yeah."

She took a large gulp of gin and put the glass down on the central island.

"Look, Eddie, you don't want to get caught up in all of this."

"No?"

"No. You're young. You took the wrong turn in life. There's still a chance..."

He leant forward and kissed her gently on the cheek.

"You're taking a fucking liberty," she said.

"The King of Kent is dead."

"All the more reason."

"Maybe it's time for the Queen of Kent to take over."

He turned to put down his glass next to hers. As she looked at the back of his neck she was possessed by a fiercely passionate intent. It all seemed so recklessly perilous. But the sense of danger brought with it a feeling of urgency rather than caution. He turned back to face her, his mouth opened slightly, as if he was about to say something. She took hold of his neck with both hands and kissed him on the lips.

"This is such a bad idea," she whispered.

"Yeah," he gasped.

Then his hands were upon her, reaching for the skin beneath her sweatshirt, his fingers strumming down along the ribcage to the waistband of her tight-fitting leggings. His hands rested on her hips, then followed the smooth curve of her buttocks. His touch was light, like a blessing.

Her caress was harder, more insistent. She clawed at his firm chest, pressed her mouth against his. She pulled away with a harsh sigh.

"Come," she gasped, grabbing his wrist and pulling him out of the kitchen and through to the living area.

When they reached the large, cream, suede sofa, she stopped and let him nuzzle against the back of her neck. He reached around to cradle her breasts, feeling her nipples stiffen in his palms. She arched her back and pushed her arse against his crotch. He groaned. Then she turned to face him once more, pulling off her top, unfastening her bra.

He slowly peeled down her yoga bottoms until he was kneeling at her feet. As she gently stroked his head, he looked up at her imploringly. Then he held onto her naked thighs and began to lap at her cunt that was already wet.

Jo quivered, her hips bucking against his eager tongue. Grabbing him by the hair she guided him back into a standing position. She pulled off his shirt, unbuckled his belt.

He danced a clumsy two-step as he rid himself of his jeans and briefs, his socks and trainers. Then he stood before her naked, poised. His hands open and his cock proud. She took hold of the shaft, and lowering herself onto the sofa, gently pulled him down on top of her.

"Fuck me," she commanded in a soft, insistent whisper.

She stretched out along the soft hide of the couch, wrapping her legs around his haunches as they coupled. They became one creature that turned and twisted, finding ever new lineaments of gratified desire. As his movements became more urgent, Jo pulled him down and rolled on top of him. As she straddled him, he reached up to grab her buttocks, and she guided him in once more. She rode him hard, chasing her own pleasure as she felt him ready to come.

"Yes," she hissed and panted out the rhythm of pure delight.

He cried out from the depths of his soul, his entire being lost within her, consumed by pure lust. And she too gave in to that blissful oblivion. Shuddering with seismic joy, she came as fiercely as she had all those years ago on that terrible night.

For some time, she lay on top of him, their bodies entwined, a perfect fit. She cradled his head as he suckled gently at her breasts. This moment would last forever, she thought. And though she knew that this was utter foolishness, nothing else mattered anymore.

She rolled over to lie next to him, and they fell into a deep slumber, a long and dreamless sleep. She woke to hear the clatter of Fraser's paws on the kitchen tiles, then their soft pad on the carpet as he trotted over to inspect this new domestic arrangement. The dog sniffed at the body that lay prone against his mistress. He caught the tang of sex and sweat and let out a short yelp.

Eddie opened his eyes and looked blearily at her.

"Hey," he whispered, and kissed her on the lips.

"We better get up."

"Yeah." He held her. "And then what?"

"Come on. Craig could be back any minute."

"I mean it, Jo."

"What?"

"About working for you."

"OK. But take it easy. We've got to be bloody careful."

"Who is this Spinks guy?"

"Never you mind."

"A gangster?"

Jo laughed softly.

"Oh, no," she said. "Much more dangerous. A policeman."

"Fuck."

"Yeah. Now look, you say you want to work for me?"

"I do."

"Then don't ask too many questions."

She got up from the couch and started to dress. She picked up his jeans, fished his mobile out of them and handed it to him.

"Here. Tell me your number, and I'll text you. Then we can stay in touch. Now put your clothes on."

He dressed as she tapped out a message. The front gate buzzer went.

"Fuck," Jo said. "That's him now."

Later that night, she curled up in bed with her phone. She found his number and typed: Hi, it's Jo.

A reply came back quickly: I want you.

Meet me tomorrow?

Yes, where?

In town. Notting hill. I'll text you the address tomorrow.

She put her mobile on the bedside table and pulled the covers over her. As she drifted off, she thought about Eddie's body next to hers. But when she slept, she was with Lee again. She dreamt of the night he had heard the noise in the garden and had gone out to confront the trespasser. She woke up in a cold sweat, and it took her a few moments to orientate herself in time, to realise that she was not stuck reliving that night, hearing the struggle outside and waiting for Lee to return with his fearful news. Yet, she felt something deep inside her, an obscure yet familiar impulse that reminded her of that very moment long ago.

11

"So, she's got a meeting with Brian Colby at his house at six o'clock? Any other communication with him?" Spinks asked.

"Wait a minute, Ray," Terry Rice replied.

"What?"

They were at the office in Terry's flat. It was cluttered with all kinds of mobile phones and a complicated stack of computer servers. The hacker had been going through what they had gleaned from Jo Royle's phone.

"This is high-grade intel," Terry went on. "And not easily obtained. I'm not sure I should be letting you have it so cheap."

"I gave you that story. What did you get for it?"

"Twenty large, like you said. And like I said, small change compared with what you're going after here."

"I don't know what the fuck you're talking about."

"The missing money from the Tunbridge Wells Job."

"What?"

"Don't act all innocent with me, Ray. I know Royle had it hidden away somewhere."

"Terry."

"And I know you've got away it with for all these years, but I'm not stupid. You're onto something big, and I want a bit of it, if you don't mind."

"What do you mean?"

"I mean more than twenty-fucking-grand."

"How about fifty?"

"I was thinking of one million."

"What? Don't be ridiculous."

"I'm serious. For retaining my services. It'll be worth it in the long run."

"Hmm. Well, the highest I can go for that is one hundred thousand."

"That's not enough. I need some proper capital."

Spinks frowned.

"So, what are *you* up to?" he demanded.

Terry sighed.

"Look, Ray. I'm going to appeal to your better nature – if that's possible. You noticed I was looking a bit butch yesterday."

"Yes."

"Well, you were witnessing the beginnings of the new me. I'm planning another big life change."

"What? But you've already done that, haven't you? Transitioned, or whatever they call it."

"That was a long time ago."

"So, what, you need some more surgery or something?"

"Yes, I do, Ray. Because I'm changing again. I'm de-transitioning."

"*De*-transitioning?"

"Well, actually it'll be more like re-transitioning. I'm not going back, I'm going forward."

"Now, you've lost me."

"I want to be a man again, Ray. And it's going to cost me a fortune."

"Oh, for fuck's sake." The Commander broke into derisive laughter.

"I didn't expect you to understand," Terry muttered bitterly. "I just thought I'd give you the chance."

"For what?"

"To behave like a decent human being."

"To understand?"

"Yes. Why not?"

"Because it's crazy. You really expect people to understand this?"

"No. I understand the world only too well. And I don't expect it to repay the compliment. I just want what's due me."

"What?" Spinks sneered. "Another sex-change operation?"

"Gender-reassignment surgery, if you don't mind. There's over ten million missing from the Tunbridge robbery. Ten percent should cover my expenses."

"I think you're getting above yourself, here. I'm willing to go up to 100K. If I can retain your services."

"I need more. Look, help me out here. You can afford it."

"I don't think so, Terry. And frankly, I think you need a different kind of help."

"What?" Terry was suddenly possessed by a cold fury. "You think I'm fucking mentally ill or something?"

"Well, first you want to change from man to woman, now you want to go back again. It does seem a little strange."

"Becoming a woman was just part of the process."

"What?"

"Now I've got to become a man again."

"Jesus. Why?"

"Because it's what I am. It's my fate. I can see the future; you know that, don't you?"

Terry took off the dark glasses and aimed a face at Ray

Spinks who looked back with a curious frown and a sudden swell of unease.

"Not this again," Spinks winced, as if he'd tasted something sour.

"Clairvoyance. Second sight; it's real, Ray. I know you don't believe it, but it is. And it's a curse more than a gift."

"Really?"

"Everything becomes so fucking predictable. There's no greater disappointment in life than having seen it all before."

"I wouldn't mind knowing what was going to happen."

"Yes, you would. You don't want to know the future, Ray."

For a moment, the Commander's gaze was held by two milky-blue and sightless orbs. They seemed to look right through him. He gave a little shudder.

"You're a fucking nutter, Terry," he muttered.

"Go on, get out! Get out of my flat!"

When Spinks had gone, Terry went through the brief flurry of texts that had been exchanged between Jo Royle and an unidentified number late last night. Yes, Spinks would pay for this, they decided. For his refusal to share in the loot but also for his humiliating manner. Terry would take their revenge for being treated like some sort of freak. They hacked into the unidentified caller's phone and began that intricate process whereby any given number could be "reversed", breaking a code that could soon reveal the name and full profile of its user.

12

It was later that morning when Eddie received the call. His mobile came to life and his heart leapt at the thought that it might be Jo. He glanced at the screen: No Caller ID, it read. He wasn't sure if it was such a good idea to answer it, but curiosity overcame caution.

"Hello?" he said.

"Eddie?" came a hoarse tone. "Eddie Pierce?"

"Who is this?"

"Call me Terry."

"And who would that be?"

"Somebody who might just be able to help you on your way."

"On my way?"

"Through the labyrinth, Eddie. Because that's where you're headed."

"Is it, now?"

"Oh, yes. There're things you need to know. Things that need to be done, too. We can work together."

"Really," Eddie sighed, now convinced he was the victim of a crank call.

"We should meet up."

"I don't think so, mate. In fact, I think I should put the phone down."

"Well, since you're seeing Jo Royle later..."

"What?"

"Oh, that got your attention, didn't it? Yes, you'd be surprised what I know about you. And I have some useful information. About Lee Royle and Ray Spinks."

Spinks, thought Eddie, that name again.

"Yes," the voice went on. "You'll be coming into town to see Jo, so we could meet up beforehand."

"Where?"

"Soho. You could buy me lunch. There's a rather nice restaurant on Greek Street called L'Escargot."

"I'm just a tipster, Eddie," Terry declared as they shared a rare Chateaubriand and a bottle of Fleurie at a corner table. "A huckster, a hustler. Selling stories, blagging confidential information, hacking into people's private lives. I'm not a very good person, some might say."

Terry rolled their cloudy eyes and Eddie laughed softly, already half-charmed by the strange creature that had summoned him. He had been unnerved by Terry's blindness at first, but in the low light of the restaurant, he felt some comfort of anonymity, that in not being visible to his lunch companion he was somehow hidden from the world. A bright day outside, but here they communed with an intimacy of night, the darkness of the confessional. Out of sight. Eyeless in Soho.

"But I'm the best there is," Terry went on. "The best there ever was. Why? Because I'm part of a tradition. There's always been people like me. Someone to mediate between the past and the future so that humanity can communicate with what lies beyond. I'm a messenger, if you like. Between this world and the underworld. With secret knowledge of the unseen."

"Right." Eddie nodded and took a sip of wine.

"I note your scepticism, young man. I don't blame you. But look at me."

Terry fixed the young man's gaze with a sightless glare.

"No," they insisted, "really look at me. What do you see with that twenty-twenty vision of yours?"

"Er…"

"Come on, don't be bashful. What do I look like?"

Eddie shrugged.

"I don't know," he mused cautiously. "Er, non-binary?"

"Hah! These quaint terms they're forever coming up with. And you have to be so careful what you say these days. I once tweeted that that I'd found I enjoyed sex better as a woman than as a man. You should have seen the trouble that brought me. God knows what they're going to think about my next move. But I'm straying from the point. The point is, Eddie, I live on the edge. I mean, I'm on the edge of the edge. And that gives me the edge."

"The edge?"

"I can see it all. Even some of what hasn't happened already."

"Really?"

"Yes, really. And I'm willing to share some of it with you."

"Some of it?"

"Listen." Terry's hand crept across the white-clothed table to pat Eddie's gently. "It will all seem a bit cryptic; that's the nature of it. And I can't tell you everything. That's not how it works."

"Sounds like a cop-out."

"It's for your own protection, believe me."

"I've heard that one before. I want to know everything."

"Of course you do. But trust me, sometimes wisdom brings no profit."

"I don't get it."

Terry sighed heavily and patted Eddie's hand one last time.

"No, I doubt if you ever will. But try to remember this: there are some things best not knowing about."

"I'll bear that in mind."

"Please do."

"In the meantime" – Eddie cleared his throat – "you said you have some information for me."

"Yes. What do you know about the Tunbridge Wells Cash Depot Robbery?"

Eddie had read about the heist in some true crime book he'd got from the library at Feltham.

"A big job, wasn't it?" he mused. "They got away with about thirty million in notes. The gang took the manager and his family hostage and forced him to get them through the security procedures of the depot to where the money was."

"Yes, what's known in the trade as a 'tiger kidnapping' – where one abducts people and by threats makes them commit a crime on your behalf. They pretended to be police and stopped the manager as he was driving to work. Then they picked up his wife and kid. Nasty business."

"Yeah."

"Setting someone up like that to rob a place. Ruthless. Thing is, Eddie, the whole thing was a setup."

"What do you mean?"

"I mean the gang that did it, they were set up to fail. Not with the robbery itself, but afterwards, when all the money was taken and ready to be divvied up. The people behind it all were in complete control. The poor fuckers who actually did the heist all get picked up within a week of the robbery. On information supplied by the very people who had organised it."

"Why?"

"Because then, everybody's happy. The case seems solved, with all the gang arrested and a big haul of the loot recovered, nearly twenty million. Kent Police are well chuffed, something of a career-making operation for some of the officers involved. And the real villains are ecstatic. They've got the remaining ten mil to sit on while everything slowly goes quiet on the case."

"And none of the actual robbers point the finger?"

"Well, what do you think? Besides, none of the gang knows who's really running things except the leader, Chris Ipsworth. And it's him that ends up getting tagged as the so-called mastermind. Nonsense, really. I mean, Chris is a game villain and all that, but no way he could have planned and ran something as big as that. And he's a bit of a mystery himself, is our Chris."

"How do you mean?"

"Well, to most people, Ipsworth is as scary as fuck. Violent and volatile. Good at hurting people and ready to take anything thrown at him. He did mixed martial arts at professional level and could have gone somewhere with that if he hadn't got caught up in all of this. And he's useful to have fronting a gang doing a heist like this where you have to act cruel and frighten people. But, by all accounts, around Lee Royle, Chris Ipsworth would turn into a complete pussycat. No one was quite sure why."

"Right."

"Anyway, he goes away as the big boss on the robbery

and Kent CID are satisfied. Flying Squad aren't so sure. They've got involved by now and think that Kent have moved too fast and just gone for the easy wins. That they should have sat back a bit and maybe watched the team that did the job lead them to the bigger guys. They've got their own operation and they're running surveillance on a certain party, and they send someone in to bug up his big mansion in the country."

"Lee Royle?"

"That's right. But that's when they really fuck up. The undercover guy is in combat fatigues and a bloody balaclava when Royle finds him on his property. So when he stabs the poor bastard, he's able to put up a self-defence plea and convince a jury. He's got a bloody clever lawyer, of course, and a bit of help from someone inside the Met."

"This Spinks guy?"

"Right again. You see, it was their job from the off. The last big one for the both of them. And they weren't too greedy. Just ten million split both ways. Let police and thieves fight over the lion's share of the loot; they were businessmen of the first order, well-practised at keeping quiet and letting others take the fall. And they had a quick and easy way of putting their portion somewhere safe. But with a policeman dead, they had to be very careful about how they would finally divide the spoils. Very, very patient. And Lee had to go away for a bit anyway."

"He got away with the killing."

"Yeah, but they managed to link him to the handling of some of the money. A bit of a trumped-up charge, but they made sure he served five out of a seven-year sentence. Royle knew he needed to do some time, given the circumstances. And he was ready to wait. Then they wait some more.

Nearly twenty years later, the Serious Fraud Office and the insurers still can't find where it's gone."

"Offshore somewhere?"

"Yes, and moving around with a complicated audit trail that links to, well, who knows where? The thing is, Eddie, money laundering doesn't happen in any particular jurisdiction, it happens between them. And if you're lucky, it keeps accumulating as you move it around. So Spinks has been determined to sit it out too, to serve his time and retire gracefully. To fool them all. I think that's as important to him as the money itself. Though, he might have got impatient."

"What do you mean?"

"Maybe he wanted to cash in his pension early."

"What, and have Lee Royle killed?"

"Wouldn't put it past him. But whatever happened, now that Royle's dead, he's going to have to make a move."

"And so, I follow him. Right?"

Terry gave a flat, mirthless laugh.

"If you can find the way in."

"What?"

"As I said, to the labyrinth. Find out where they first hid the money. An island somewhere. It could be Cayman, the British Virgin Islands. Or closer to home, one of the Crown Dependencies, perhaps."

"Like, you mean, Jersey or something?"

"Yes, but be careful, young man. Several people have been done away with because they got too close to this for Spinks's liking. He's a cold-blooded bastard that likes to play tricks with his victims."

"Yeah?"

"Oh, yeah. He likes to confuse people, to put them off balance so they give away what they know. And he likes riddles. Some say it was an advanced technique in cognitive interrogation developed at Bramshill Police College. Others, that it was a trick he picked up from Popeye Doyle in *The French Connection*."

"What's that?"

"A film in the 1970s. Gene Hackman plays this narcotics detective, and in the middle of grilling a suspect he'll ask them something weird like 'did you pick your feet in Poughkeepsie?' to disorient them. But I think Ray Spinks just likes to fuck with people. And there's one puzzle that keeps coming up: 'what walks on four legs in the morning, two legs at noon, and three legs in the evening?'"

"I think I know that one. It's 'man', isn't it?"

"Very good. Oldest one in the book, of course. It's about humanity, Eddie. How we progress through life. The child crawling, the adult walking, the old man limping with a stick. Everyone's a puzzle, of course. So be careful who you trust."

Eddie thought for a moment.

"What about Jo Royle?"

"Even her."

"Yeah?

"Yeah. She's got her secrets like everybody else. Remember, all riddles are there to be solved. Except one."

"And what's that?

"Our own. The riddle of the self. That one we really shouldn't try. I'm proof positive of that."

"Doesn't make sense."

"No, but that's the very riddle of life, Eddie."

13

Forget this rotten world; and unto thee,
Let thine own times as an old story be.

Brian Colby recalled these lines from the opening stanza of John Donne's "Of the Progress of the Soul" and felt a swooning sense of relief. It was true, then, he told himself: Lee Royle was really dead. So it was all over. All these years of fear, guilt, and anxiety could be finally coming to an end. As he walked to his car, he was possessed by an almost metaphysical euphoria of wellbeing.

He lifted the sealed padded A4 envelope he had retrieved from the safe deposit box and held it up to his face for a moment, as if it were an icon to be kissed. Then he placed it on the passenger seat and put his seatbelt on. He had waited to be rid of this thing for nearly twenty years. The curse on his life that he could now put behind him.

It was never meant to be like this, he thought as he drove home to Notting Hill. His life, it had taken a wrong turn long ago. But there was yet time to put it all right again.

Brian Colby had been such a promising young man. He'd studied English Literature at Warwick University and had written a brilliant dissertation on the Metaphysical Poets. He had been happiest then, a shining light in a group of clever and witty people. Sex and drugs were freely indulged in, and there was always the promise of intelligent conversation. A "perfect balance of the sensual and the cerebral", he'd once announced at an utterly decadent weekend party. He had somehow thought this life would go on forever.

But once he graduated, most of his circle had paired off and settled down. He wanted more of that stimulating life he had known at college. He found a cheap flat in Brixton with some notion that he was going to write something. But nothing came. He drifted in and out of a series of dull jobs. There wasn't much out there for an expert in John Donne and Andrew Marvell.

He started volunteering at the local law centre. He had principles back then. Working with asylum seekers, housing and human rights issues, he thought he'd found some sort of a cause for a while. He did a post-graduate law degree and found he had a talent for criminal cases and miscarriages of justice. And that's when his life started to go bad.

At first, there had been some simple, worthy cases to defend. Small and petty injustices that nonetheless ruined the lives of the ordinary people caught up in them. He found that he could be useful, make a difference. But even back then, he started to develop an expertise in the technicalities of the law rather than its principles.

A big drugs case came his way. The police had clearly overstepped the mark in the way they had dealt with the defendants. This was a great opportunity to address some serious irregularities, to bring the authorities to book, he reasoned. Colby was keyed up. Excited about the case, overconfident in his powers and, worst of all, a little self-righteous about his role. As he imagined himself somehow above it all, he allowed his glamorous new clients to get close to him when he should have kept them at a professional distance. He'd acquired a considerable cocaine habit by then, which gave him that dangerous illusion of control just at the point when he had started to lose it.

At the time, it seemed a gradual, barely perceptible shift towards damnation. Even when one of the gangsters he was defending showed him a secret video he'd taken showing Colby snorting coke with a couple of hookers, the lawyer still imagined that this was an elaborate game that he could argue his way out of. A balance of the sensual and the cerebral that he'd known from his university days. But he soon learnt that this new predicament was far from academic. He was now tainted and in the control of bad forces. And he had yet further to fall, a long slow vertiginous descent.

He found his services retained by organised crime figures as his practice and principles became ever more compromised. By the time he started working for Lee Royle, he had become utterly corrupt, resigned to the fact that society was rotten to the core. Donne's poetry, that he had once loved, now haunted him. *The world is but a carcass; thou art fed/ by it, but as a worm that carcass bred.*

He had all the trappings of a successful life. But what an apt term that was: trappings. A vulgar wealth that merely confirmed how cheaply he had sold his soul. A townhouse on Kensington Park Gardens, full of expensive things. A life of bought pleasure, an exquisite collection of first editions, the Mercedes-Benz C-Class Saloon he was cruising along in. All a lot of tinsel, really. Scant consolation for a sullied career, a failed marriage, and the lack of any true friends he could really trust.

With the Tunbridge Wells Job, he'd dealt with the legal side of things for Lee's defence, making sure that he wasn't able to be placed in any financial link with it. Royle himself was very careful that these things needed to be compartmentalised. Colby tried to remain blissfully ignorant of any of the complicated money laundering schemes that wound around that business. He had seen too many people killed or put away for years over it. But for all his care and caution, he still knew too much for his own good.

There was the envelope lying in the safe deposit box, waiting for the occasion of Lee Royle's death so that it could be delivered. The danger of its possession had haunted him, even as he had tried to make his practice more legitimate, to pass on nefarious work to younger lawyers keen for the spoils of wickedness. Now he could be rid of it and free of its legacy. He could start his life again. Forget this rotten world.

He would sell off his firm. Maybe try and find somewhere that he could do the good work once more. Redeem himself. In the meantime, he would take a sabbatical. He would write. Yes. What stories he would have to tell!

And he would have time to read again. To find solace in poetic reflection as he had as a young man. He had already started to go back to the books that had once so inspired him. Only yesterday, he had taken down his copy of John Donne's *Devotions Upon Emergent Occasions*, a rare second edition in its original calfskin binding that he had bought at auction for five thousand pounds. Donne had written this series of meditations whilst struggling to get over a debilitating illness. A sickness that he saw as a rebuke from God for sinfulness. It was a discourse on recovery, and Colby now saw it as a guide to his own. It would help him give up his bad ways. It would help him to get better.

He was already thinking of it as he let himself into his house. It was lying in wait for him on the coffee table, with a notebook and pen at the ready. He was so preoccupied that he scarcely noticed the looseness of the lock on the front door.

He wandered into the kitchen. Put his briefcase on the table and his mobile phone next to it. He slipped out the dreaded envelope, put it under his arm. Checking the fridge, he found an open bottle of Sancerre. He poured himself a glass and went through to the drawing room.

He took a gulp of wine and sighed as he entered his lavish, book-lined chamber. He hadn't felt this happy in years. This would be his refuge now. But as he walked across toward the marble fireplace, he saw something that gave his whole body a horrible, sickening start. Someone was sitting on the oxblood Chesterfield facing the window.

It was Ray Spinks.

"Hello, Brian," he said in a smoothly threatening tone.

"Jesus," Colby felt the envelope slip out of his armpit onto the floor.

"Sorry for the, er, intrusion. You know, you should really upgrade the security on this place."

"What are you doing here?"

"I know. I should have made an appointment. Very naughty of me just barging in like this. But what are you going to do? Call the police?"

Spinks gave a mirthless grin, his mouth twisted in a ghastly rictus. The eyes coldly vigilant, though. It was then that Colby noticed that his visitor was wearing surgical gloves and blue plastic overshoes.

"Ray," he croaked.

"Take a seat, Brian," Spinks motioned to the armchair opposite him and then leant over to pick up what had been dropped. "Is this what I think it is?"

"Listen," Colby tried to reason as he sat down.

"Shh," Spinks insisted, and broke the seal on the package. "Let's have little look, shall we?"

He slid out a sheaf of documents, tossed the envelope onto the sofa and began to leaf through the paperwork slowly.

"You know what this is, right?" Spinks peered up at Colby.

"I don't know anything; really, Ray. I was just instructed to hold it in a secure place for my client."

"And you were going to hand this over to that bitch Jo Royle?"

"Well, it's yours now Ray, isn't it?"

"Yes, it is."

"Then…then…everything's OK. Isn't it?"

"Ah, but you can see my problem now, can't you Brian? I can't have too many people knowing about this."

"I told you. I've never known the contents of that envelope. Honest to God."

"But you can see this puts me in a difficult position. I need to know that you don't know. Don't I?"

"Yes, but…"

"So, let's have a little guessing game, shall we?"

"No need for that, Ray."

"What creature walks on four legs in the morning? Two legs at noon…"

"Please, don't do this."

"…and three legs in the evening. Hmm, last one's a bit of a clue, isn't it?"

"I wouldn't know."

"Of course you do, Brian," Spinks pulled out a pistol and pointed it at Colby. "You're an educated man. Come on, tell me."

"Well, it's, it's 'man'."

"Why?"

"Why?"

"Yes, why? Why is it 'man'?"

"It's how we go through life – a baby walking on its arms and legs, an adult on two legs, an old person walking with a stick."

"But what does that mean?"

"What?"

"Man. What's the significance of that?"

"Come on, Ray, please…"

Spinks gestured with the gun.

"Tell me. What does 'man' mean?"

"I don't know, it's, it's…" Colby struggled for some sort of convincing answer. "Humanity? The progress we make through our existence? Mortality?"

"You were always a clever cunt, Brian. Too clever, I think."

"Look, I don't know what it means. I don't know what 'man' means."

"I don't believe you."

The lawyer knew that it would be fatal to tell the policeman what he really knew. His mind grasped desperately for something to say. But he had run out of ideas.

"Please, Ray," he begged. "I really don't know."

"Sorry, Brian. Maybe you don't. But I can't take the risk."

And with that, Spinks shot Colby through the heart.

He blacked out for about thirty seconds. When he came to, he found himself on the floor, slumped over the coffee table. Blood was pumping out of his chest, drenching his expensive Persian carpet, the antique kilim with the beautiful *elibelinde* motif he had found in a shop on the Portobello Road ten years before. The bemusement he felt in finding that he was still alive was tempered by a dread that he didn't have much time left.

He heard his mobile ring in the kitchen. He tried to get up but found he could only move his head and his right arm. Ray Spinks had gone, his line of vision was limited, but he was certain of that. If only he could get to his phone. He struggled to push himself up, but he slipped back down onto the tabletop, his face close to the leather spine of the John Donne volume he had been so keen to get back to that day.

And as he listened to the ring tone, a passage of that work came to him, from its most famous part. "Meditation XVII" with its opening: *Now this bell tolling softly for another says to me, Thou must die.* He shuddered in bitter laughter. Blood began to fill his mouth. But in his last moments, he had an inspiration. A clue he could leave behind, if only he had enough strength.

He grabbed the book and leafed through to that section. A well-thumbed page, thank God, not hard to find. He flattened the book out with his arm and reached for the pen next to it. He was struggling to breath now, and pain surged through his body. But this last thought kept him going. He would write something, after all. Or at least make a mark. Leave a message.

Because Spinks was right, he did know what the riddle really meant, and now he could pass that on. He took the pen and, hovering it over a well-known line in the middle of the passage, lowered the nib gently to make a single scratch. A comma, yes, that would do it, he thought. Just a bit of punctuation. Grammatical particle physics: one tiny quantum of information that could change the meaning a line completely. And poetic justice for Ray Spinks, he hoped as he took his last breath. For the man had surely punctuated him. With a hole in the heart. A full stop.

14

It took Ray Spinks twenty minutes to get back to his office where he had left a small carry-on suitcase next to his desk. He sat down and looked through the document he had taken from Brian Colby. He opened his laptop and searched for a company online and logged in using an ID and password he found in the paperwork. As he activated an account, he made a phone call and tried to schedule a meeting. A date was arranged, and Spinks was told that they would phone him back later to confirm. He then closed his computer and slipped it and the document into his briefcase.

He looked around his office, and at the view beyond the window from the fifth floor of New Scotland Yard. He was going to miss being in the Job, that was for sure. He had loved being a policeman, and he knew that he'd been good at it. In his own way, of course. He had managed to keep the lid on crime in his day. To contain it. That's what all the do-gooders failed to understand: that you could never completely eradicate crime or vice. Get rid of one set of gangsters and another lot will just fill the gap. You have to regulate it. Make terms with it, if you had to. And he had always loved the power that had given him.

He looked down at his desk and the fat slab of bureaucracy that still squatted there. The report he had been slaving over for all this time, still waiting for his attention after the last notes from the Deputy Assistant Commissioner. He reached down to pull over a wastepaper bin and scooped the heavy volume into it. There was a satisfying thud as he filed the wretched thing away for good.

This is what the Job had become: a mess of bureaucracy, a series of exercises in box-ticking. And he was glad he was putting that behind him. He checked his watch. He would have to get a move on. He needed to get to London City Airport within the hour.

As he came out of the lift, he pulled the handle up on his suitcase and towed it behind him as he made his way out. The little wheels made a satisfying drone as they trundled along the smooth floor. A holiday sound. And he was in a vacational mood. The surge of adrenaline from killing his prey now faded into a buzz of sheer relief. His consciousness flooded with that sublime feeling: of having gotten away with it.

Lee Royle's death had proved fortuitous, smoking out his widow's legacy and giving him twice the reward he had originally bargained for. And with Colby gone, there was now nothing that could link him directly to the Tunbridge Wells Job and the missing millions.

His glory would trail him, of being such a clever bastard. He glowed inside with all the secret knowledge he had taken from the world. Now, this was his greatest riddle, and with it he had fooled them all.

His mobile went and he fished it out of his jacket pocket. It was confirmation of his appointment. But they needed the ID and password details from the document. He stopped in the foyer and cradled the phone between his ear and shoulder and fumbled at his briefcase, opening it with one hand, pulling out the sheaf of paper with the other.

"Just a minute," he muttered into the phone.

Looking up, he saw a young woman come through the entrance and approach him. And he realised that it was that detective constable who had come to see him about the Royle killing. *Fuck*, he thought and felt the phone slip. But as he grabbed at it, he let the document fall on the floor in front of him, just as the woman reached him.

"Can I call you back," he said and ended the call.

He went to pick up what he had dropped but she beat him to it, slowly rising from a crouch with it in her hands. *Fuck*, he thought again, holding her gaze, desperately willing her not to look at what she held in her hands.

"Commander Spinks," she said with a smile.

"Yes. It's Detective Constable…"

"Hussain."

"Of course." He put the phone into his jacket pocket and quickly grabbed the document with his free hand. "How's the investigation?"

He continued to try fix her with a stare as he took it from her.

"Got a call from someone claiming to be an eyewitness. Claimed the assailant was driving a red sports car."

It was then that she tried to get a proper look at the paperwork as he bundled it into his briefcase.

"Really?"

"Yeah. Except we can't trace the call, and they didn't call back. I was wondering if we could have a word, sir."

"Not the best time, I'm afraid." He fastened the case and reached around to pick up the handle of the carry-on bag. "You really should have made an appointment."

"I did try to. I was told you're going on leave. Thought I'd try and catch you before you went away."

"Right."

"Going somewhere nice?"

"You could say that," he countered, knowing that he had to make sure she didn't know his destination.

There was an awkward moment as she waited for him to say something more. He gave a mirthless grin.

"I'm in a bit of a hurry, to tell you the truth," he told her.

"Just a couple of things. I'll walk you to your car."

"OK," he sighed, and they made their way out of the building together. "This victim profile thing, is it?"

"Well, to be frank, sir, I'm worried about operational security."

"What do you mean?"

"The leak to the press, for one thing. That could have compromised the whole investigation."

"Someone on your team being a bit naughty?"

"I don't think so, sir. I think we're pretty tight."

"That's good to know."

"So, if you have any thoughts on how it might have happened?"

"What?"

"Well, you were the only other person informed of the identity of the victim."

"Now, wait a minute. Are you implying that I might have had something to do with it?"

"I'm just asking, sir."

"You want to be careful, making accusations. The next thing you know you'll be saying I had something to do with the murder."

"Well, did you?"

Spinks laughed.

"Oh, you're too good for me, Detective Constable. Oh, yes, you've caught me out."

"You did have a relationship with the victim, sir."

"You're bold. I'll give you that. But I mean it. Be careful. If you want to get on, you don't want to stir things up too much."

"I just want to get to the truth."

Spinks laughed again and turned to look up at the building they had just left.

"You think they want to get to the truth? I mean, the whole truth? Nobody does. We keep the peace; that's what we do. Look, everyone thinks I'm bent." He suddenly felt reckless in the knowledge that he would soon be far away from all of this. "But I kept the streets safe. For ordinary decent people, that is. Now, if you'll excuse me."

He started to walk away from her. Then he turned back.

"You know what the liar's riddle is?" he asked her.

"The liar's riddle?"

"Yeah. It's what's called a paradox of self-reference. Some ancient Greek from Crete came up with it."

"Is that where you're headed, sir? Crete? Or maybe Northern Cyprus?"

"Oh, you don't give up, do you? No, this is an unsolvable conundrum. And when you've been in the Job a bit longer, you might find it useful. Basically, it goes like this: I say, 'I admit I'm a liar,' right?"

"Er, yeah."

"Then I'm telling the truth about myself, aren't I?"

"I suppose so."

"Then I'm not a liar anymore, am I?"

Spinks turned his back on her and kept walking.

"Wait a minute," she called after him.

But he was gone.

15

The address Jo had texted to Eddie took him to Kensington Park Gardens, a street of elegantly stucco-fronted houses. She had said that she would meet him outside, but there was no sign of her. He checked the house number once more, then called her. As he waited for her to answer, he looked up at the cast-iron balustrade beneath the first-floor windows that ran the length of the terrace. A colonnaded portico framed a heavy front door crowned with a fanlight. This was what laundered money bought, he mused.

As the phone switched to voicemail, he ended the call and began a text. As he thought of what words to use, he climbed the stone steps in front of the entrance. He shrugged and buzzed the entry phone.

I'm here now, he typed. Where are U?

He waited. There was no reply to either. He tapped gently against the front door. It gave a little. It was on the latch.

No, he thought.

Don't go in.

This seemed some sort of trap laid for him. He knew that he should turn around and walk away. But then he would never know of what great chance might be waiting for him. He would lose his place in the game. So he pushed at the open door and walked in.

It did not take him long to find Brian Colby. The body sprawled out in a pool of blood in the drawing room, his right arm still stretched out across the coffee table, an open book trapped beneath the clawed hand. A pistol, on its side, lay next to them. He leant over to examine this curious arrangement. Again, part of his mind was screaming at him to get out, but a profound sense of curiosity drew him in. He knew that somewhere here was the key to the secrets that Terry Rice spoke of.

He spotted the manila envelope on the Chesterfield and picked it up. "For Jo Royle, to be opened on the event of my death" was written on the front. It was empty. He heard footsteps in the hallway. As the front room door opened, he grabbed the gun from the table and turned around.

"Eddie?"

"Jo."

She looked at the pistol in his hand. Pointing at her. Then she looked beyond him, to Brian Colby's bloody corpse.

"What have you done?"

"What?"

He frowned. Then he realised that this was the trap. To be found here with the dead lawyer. With the gun in his hand.

"You set me up."

"No. But you…"

The sound of a police siren howling across the streets outside cut her off. It was getting louder. Closer.

"You bitch."

"No!"

He looked at the gun in his hand. Jo gasped. He had to get rid of it, and there was no time to wipe it free of his prints, so he shoved it into his waistband and turned his back on her.

"Eddie, did you…"

"No! I found him like this. Like I was supposed to."

"This was meant for me," she insisted. "Look, you've got to get out of here."

"Come on, then." He spun around and started to walk towards the hallway, taking her arm.

"No. I've got to stay here. There are phone records of me having a six o'clock appointment with Colby. You go."

They were out by the front door.

"What, so I can be caught fleeing the crime scene with the murder weapon? Is that it?"

"Please, Eddie."

He opened the door enough so that he could peer out at the street. A BMW X5 Armed Response Vehicle screeched to a halt in front of the house.

"Fuck," he seethed, and, grabbing her once more, pushed her out across the threshold and slammed the door shut behind her.

Jo stumbled onto the doorstep as three officers came bundling out, brandishing Heckler & Koch MP5 semi-automatic carbines.

"Armed police!" the lead officer screamed at her. "Show me your hands!"

She did what she was told as he came forward.

"Turn around! Hands behind your back!" he barked as he lowered her onto the ground and two other officers raced past her to break the door down.

When they took her in for questioning and to take forensic samples, she decided that she would give them a statement. She was much more used to giving a consistent "no comment" in police interviews, but she knew it wouldn't work this time. The danger was now in giving a partial version of the events. She decided that she would tell them about her appointment with Colby but leave out any reference to Eddie. All of their communications had been on encrypted phones and there was nothing that could link them except his association with Craig. If they had him in custody and he told them something different, this could mean real trouble for her, but it was a risk she had to take. She laughed bitterly when they asked her if she wanted a lawyer present.

"My lawyer's not much use to me now, darling," she told them.

16

Eddie had made it to the first-floor landing by the time they had broken the door down. He entered a front bedroom and went up to the window as another siren sounded. Staying out of view, he peered down at the street below. Jo was face down on the pavement as an armed officer stood over her, another police vehicle pulled up outside the house.

Eddie reached over to unscrew the window lock, praying that there wasn't a more elaborate pin-lock in the casement as he pushed at the frame. The lower sash lifted, and he clenched his jaw as the old wood creaked against the side jamb, but the commotion below drowned out the noise.

He crawled out onto the balcony, wiped down any surfaces on the window he might have touched with the sleeve of his shirt, and closed it gently behind him. He huddled down on the iron frame and looked down. Jo was still on the floor. A policeman stood guard on the pavement, his head scarcely more than two yards from where Eddie crouched.

He edged his way along the walkway, holding his breath, conscious of the fact that at any sound or movement might cause the man to turn and see him. But nobody was looking up. Two more armed officers were hurrying into the house and, as a small crowd started to gather, a cordon was being set up and people ushered away by stern-voiced police.

When he reached the end, Eddie stepped over to the balcony of the adjacent house in the terrace, which gave him access to the flat roof of a colonnaded porch, from which he could shin down out of sight of the growing tumult next door. He walked down the steps casually, as if he owned the place, and made his way briskly up the road towards where his car was parked, two streets away.

He arrived at his flat in Greenhithe forty-five minutes later. It was part of a twelve-story luxury development next to the river that boasted underground parking, a ground-floor supermarket, a waterside piazza with cafés, restaurants, and bars, and eleven acres of landscaped gardens. The building itself was a high-rise steel and concrete cage, frilled with glass balustrades, panelled with white stone and grey brick facades.

He walked through the entrance lobby, past the resident's lounge area, towards the lift. There was an abstract painting in the foyer, a large symmetrical inkblot that he'd scarcely noticed before. Now it seemed to project the empty meaning of a psychological test.

Everything's a fucking puzzle, he thought to himself as he pressed the button for the elevator.

He entered his flat and closed the heavy brushed-steel door behind him. His footfalls echoed on the stained-timber flooring as he walked into the open-plan kitchen and dining area. He slapped his key fob on the composite stone worktop and savoured a moment of empty solace. Exhaling a hollow sigh, he pulled out the pistol from the waistband of his trousers and put it on the counter. He then took the other object he had taken from Colby's house and placed it next to the gun and went over to the drinks cabinet.

Pouring himself a large Remy Martin, he looked around, as if to get his bearings. Yes, he reasoned, this was where he belonged. The cold, antiseptic anonymity of a well-appointed one-bedroom apartment. With its clean lines, minimalist fittings and furniture, it was the perfect refuge from all the madness out there. The perfect hiding place from all these painful new thoughts and feelings.

He took a slug of brandy. Then another. He needed to anaesthetize his mind from all of its tormenting questions. Quell his febrile senses. He poured himself another glass and downed it in one. He wanted to kill that awful yearning that he felt for her.

He wanted to believe that she hadn't set him up. That he had walked into the trap that had been laid for her. But he couldn't be sure. He was in love – or at least, he thought he was – and that made him fatally vulnerable. He had fallen for her, but maybe that was all part of the plan.

She hadn't told him anything about the deal between Lee and Ray Spinks. She had expected him to simply follow her orders.

All he wanted to do now was forget. So, he kept drinking until his mind reached the edge of oblivion. He staggered into the bedroom and clumsily undressed. He collapsed onto the bed, a child crawling on all fours to nestle beneath the covers. How we progress through life, Terry Rice had said. Towards three-legged old age. But he wanted to go back, to regress. He curled up his body in foetal sanctuary. His mind darkened and deepened.

As it came back to the surface, many hours later, his consciousness was flooded by vivid and violent images. He awoke with a start, a thin sheen of sweat shrouding his body. In the instant he awoke, he felt possessed by a lucid horror that brought absolute clarity. Suddenly, everything made sense.

He stumbled into the bathroom and ran the cold tap in the sink. He caught his reflection in the mirror, a perplexed expression looking back. Another self, ready to question him. He wondered, and not for the first time, what had compelled him to this life? Had he been born bad? He splashed some water in his face and tried to recall his dream. But it was gone. That moment of enlightenment had just been an illusion, a trick played by the unconscious. But there was a real problem to solve now, he realised. And he would have to wake himself up properly to do that.

He padded out to the living room area with a renewed sense of purpose. He went to the lacquered wooden cabinet beneath the fifty-inch wall-mounted flatscreen television. Reaching into the back of the cabinet, he popped open a false compartment and took out what was in there. Three rolls of banknotes, amounting to £15,000, and a one-kilo slab of cocaine in plastic sealing.

He took the coke to the kitchen and, cutting it open, poured a little of the white powder on the work surface. He chopped out two fat lines and snorted them up. Then he perused the two items he had taken from Brian Colby's study.

There was the gun, a dark grey automatic. Eddie was taking a massive risk by having this in his possession, but something told him that it might come in handy. Thinking tactically, he reasoned that just as it had been left to implicate someone else, he too might be able to use it as a plant. And his survival instincts concluded that he maybe needed a gun right now himself.

He picked it up and weighed it in his palm. He would "walk heavy" now, as Jamal had put it; he would have to be ruthless. Some trace of his dream yet flickered in his thoughts. A lost memory and a prophesy of violence. He put the pistol down and picked up the other artefact.

It was the red leather-bound volume that Brian Colby had been holding. Eddie had taken it when he had turned away from Jo in the drawing room. As he wondered if it might hold some sort of secret, it struck him that the book could be every bit as deadly as the gun. He turned to that page with a marked passage that the lawyer's dead hand had pointed to and began to read.

17

Jo woke later that day with a glaring headache. The police had kept her for nearly three hours the night before, going over every detail of her statement. She had waited for the moment when they might confront her with the knowledge that Eddie had been there. She found herself second-guessing every line of enquiry that they might follow. In the end, he was never mentioned, and that had put her even more on edge. She was mentally exhausted.

She had come back late to Sevengates to find a crew of reporters plotted up by the gates. Lee's entire property had been landscaped to keep away prying eyes and to block the view of any long lens. But she hated the feeling of being under siege by the tabloid scum.

She called Craig in the afternoon. Brian Colby's killing was all over the news by now, along with much speculation about his links with Lee. Craig told her they should think about upping their security and suggested sending a couple of guys over. That was the last thing she needed.

"Look," she told him. "With all the reporters outside, we probably don't need it. For now, anyway."

"OK. But if anything comes up…"

"Don't worry. I'm going to get some rest now."

"OK. Call me if you need anything."

"Oh, and Craig?"

"What?"

She wanted to ask him about Eddie, but she feared that this might make her brother suspicious.

"Nothing," she said, and ended the call.

Jo sighed. She wanted to know more. She really needed to find out more about Eddie.

Or did she?

She really wanted to trust him but couldn't be sure if he was somehow part of Colby's murder. And that was too much of a risk to take. She didn't even know if he had been arrested or not. Maybe the best thing was to just forget about him for now. She had let herself get carried away, that was all. She poured herself a large gin and tonic and staggered into bed.

The morning came bright and unforgiving. She knew that she had to get up and start to deal with putting Lee's business affairs in order. To salvage what she could, now that his secret fortune had been stolen. She would have to get a new lawyer, that was for sure.

But all she could think about was Eddie. It had been so good. It had even felt like love, but, as usual, fate had dealt her a losing hand. She would just have to get over it. There were, after all, more serious things to worry about. She still wondered where he was and what had happened to him, but she knew that if the police had caught him, she would know about it soon enough. Perhaps he had got way. For good.

She sighed and tried to concentrate on the more serious matters at hand. But the spark of something burned at the emptiness she felt in the very pit of her being. *Fuck*, she thought. They'd had unprotected sex. Maybe this thing did have consequences, whether she liked it or not. And the thought of this took her to a very dark place.

So she called her GP practice and told the receptionist that it was an emergency. Luckily, there had been a cancellation, and they were able to give her an appointment at noon. As she was getting ready, her phone went with a number she didn't recognise on the screen. She picked it up, thinking it might be the clinic checking on something.

"Jo Royle?" came a woman's voice.

"That's me."

"Detective Constable Hussain."

Shit, she thought. *This is all I need.*

"What do you want?"

"I'm calling about the incident last night in Notting Hill."

"I gave a full statement to the investigation team."

"I know. I was just wondering if I could talk to you."

"What about?"

"About anything that might relate to your husband's murder."

"I don't know about that. You might have to wait until I've found a new lawyer."

"Fair enough."

"And I'm a little busy at the moment, so if you don't mind…"

"Just one more thing."

"What?"

"Well," Meera Hussain sighed. "Given the recent developments, it might be good to arrange some police protection for you."

Jo laughed.

"Are you serious?"

"Very much so."

"Well, don't worry yourselves. We can look after ourselves, thanks."

"Look, I know this is awkward. But maybe it could be done through Cheryl Symons?"

"Who?"

"Your family liaison officer."

"Oh, fuck off."

"I'm sorry?"

"This tired old good cop, bad cop routine. I'm not a complete cunt, you know."

"I can assure you Ms Royle, I'm not trying to…"

"And if you don't mind, I have to get on." Jo ended the call.

She tried not to feel rattled. All this talk of security and protection simply emphasised how vulnerable she was. How alone she felt. Well, she would have to face facts, she decided. Deal with things on her own terms, including what Eddie might have left her with.

So she cowled herself in a grey hooded top and a pair of black Versace butterfly sunglasses, fired up her pearl-blue Mitsubishi Shogun, and set off for Dartford. The long driveway allowed her to pick up speed, so that by the time she came through the automatic gates she was going fast enough to catch the press pack off guard. A couple of alert photographers managed to let off a few rounds and huge telephoto apertures snapped away greedily as she hared past them.

In the consulting room, the female GP asked her a series of questions about her recent sexual activity. It gave her an odd sense of validation. That something romantic had actually happened after all these years. At least she would have memories.

And the solution to her problem was simple and straightforward – though, Jo wasn't so sure.

"But I can't just take the morning after pill," she said. "We had sex the day before last."

The doctor smiled.

"It can work for up to five days after you've had sex."

"So, it's like a chemical abortion, or something?"

"Oh, no. It's not as invasive as that. It works by inhibiting the egg's release so that the sperm in the fallopian tubes won't be able to get to it."

"You mean there might be live sperm still inside me?"

"Very probably. They can live in there for five days. Look, conception happens when you ovulate, when the egg is released from the ovary. The egg decides, not the sperm. And, well, we can delay that decision."

Jo liked the sound of that. The doctor tore off the prescription and handed it to her.

She motored back along a winding B road that edged a field fluorescent yellow with rapeseed. Taking solace from a beautiful day in the Kent countryside, Jo relaxed for a moment and tried to enjoy the drive and ignore the annoying dark-blue Volvo Saloon that was tailgating her. She sighed sadly as she thought of Eddie once more. Part of him still alive within her. A great fleet of his seed navigating a perilous strait, seeking the refuge only one might find. A microscopic odyssey that would be brought to an end by the foil and plastic blister pack in her handbag.

When she reached a wider part of the road, she slowed down to let the Volvo overtake. But as it did so, blue lights flashed in its radiator grill and on the windscreen above the dashboard. A siren ululated. It was an unmarked police car that now pulled up in front of her. A plainclothes officer jumped out and raced to where she was parked.

"Kent CID," he announced urgently, flashing an ID fob at her. "You've got to come with us now."

"What's all this about?"

"We're here to protect you."

"Look," she insisted, getting out of her jeep. "I told Detective Constable Hussain I didn't want any fucking protection."

This seemed to throw him a little, but he took her arm and ushered her toward the Volvo.

"We've intelligence of an imminent threat to your life."

He opened a back door of the Saloon and took the keys of the Mitsubishi from her.

"What fucking threat?" she protested as he pushed her into the passenger seat.

"This threat, you bitch," came the voice of a man sitting next to her as he pushed the barrel of an automatic pistol against the side of her cheek.

He laughed and pulled the gun away from her so that she could turn and look at him. She gasped in recognition at the pale-brown features, still handsome though battered by years in the fight game. He fixed her with his sad blue eyes, his full mouth widened in a malicious grin. It was Chris Ipsworth.

18

The hotel bar was full of bikers getting drunk. A legion of red faces and bad haircuts with pint glasses aloft, triumphantly raucous. It was as if some archaic army had come to sack the city: helmets, leather jackets, and gauntlets cluttered the floor like discarded war gear. Spinks noted some gang colours as he headed towards the reception desk. "HOUNDS OF HADES MC 1%" emblazoned around a flaming dog skull on a denim cut-off.

They all seemed rapt in inebriated ritual: breaking out in sudden chants, gestures, sung snatches of heavy metal songs. Yet they made room for him as he weaved his way through, lurching at him with vehement greetings and friendly grimaces. They were happy barbarians. Humdrum souls wired into some atavistic mindset for the weekend. Belligerent without malice, all aggression played out in affectation and display.

At the desk, he caught the eye of the harassed hotel manager who gave him an ingratiating smile and came over.

"Mr Brown," the man said, using the alias Spinks had given when he had checked in. "Let me guess, you're looking for somewhere quiet for lunch."

"You've read my mind," Spinks smiled.

"Well, it is Mad Sunday."

"Mad Sunday?"

"Yes. Right in the middle of the fortnight. The first week is for practice, the second is race week. In between, you have Mad Sunday. Everyone is allowed on the course."

"Like running with the bulls?"

"What?"

"You know, Pamplona, Spain. They let the spectators run with the bulls before a fight. A bit of danger for the punters."

"Yeah, that's it. Thing is, there's hardly any trouble. They're loud and boisterous, but there's never any real aggro."

"Of course not. A whiff of death makes everybody cheerful."

"Sorry?" the manager frowned.

"If a sport is really dangerous, then the crowd is more likely to be well behaved. Take football, for instance. A soft game."

"Really?"

"Oh, yeah. Not nearly enough violence on the pitch."

The man laughed, but Spinks was warming to his theme. Remembering the gruesome Saturday afternoons on duty at Stamford Bridge in the 1970s, when he was still in uniform.

"That's why you get hooligans, you see?" he went on. "They get bored. Not enough excitement in the game itself. It's the element of real danger that's missing in this day and age. People want blood. That's what the Romans understood. If you ask me, *real* sport is where there's a possibility of death. You know what I mean? Boxing, bullfighting, and, of course, motor racing. It's the real prospect of somebody getting topped that keeps everybody happy, isn't it?"

"Er, yes," the manager forced a smile.

"Sorry," Spinks shrugged. "Somewhere for lunch?"

"Of course. There's a quiet little French place. Tucked away in one of the back streets. About a twenty-minute walk. I'll show you where it is on the map."

Outside was a bestiary of customised machinery. Grandiose chrome-work and lurid paint jobs. Comic book sci-fi and Gothic fantasies of some long-lost future. He blinked against the June sunlight and the sting of wind coming off the sea as a parade of motorbikes did wheelies along the promenade. They were right about crowd control. Just a handful of white-helmeted local woodentops, and some stewards in orange hi-vis, kept watch on the boozy mob behind the crash barriers. There was a carnival atmosphere, a spirit of folk revelry.

Mad Sunday: yes, he liked the sound of that. A true bacchanalia, with its own solemn blood-rite. And his instincts concluded that there would indeed be death in the afternoon. The scent of it hung in the air amid the fumes of petrol and engine oil. Maybe, like Terry Rice, he was having some sort of premonition. A sacrifice was needed, after all; he suddenly felt certain of that. Something to placate the gods for the great fortune that would soon be his. A senseless smash-up, he mused eagerly. A horrible and needless accident, preferably after lunch; that would do it.

At the restaurant, he finished off a confit de canard and a bottle of burgundy. He was in a holiday mood and mused idly on his impending retirement. The waiter approached.

"Would sir care to see the dessert menu?" he asked.

"Yes." Spinks wiped his mouth with his napkin. "Sir, would. Wait."

He called the man back.

"Yes?"

"Here's one for you."

"What?"

"A little conundrum."

"Sir?"

"A riddle. What's this?" Spinks wagged a forefinger at the frowning waiter. "The man who made it doesn't want it. The man who bought it doesn't need it. The man who uses it doesn't know it."

The waiter smiled and gave a little shrug.

"I give up, sir."

"Yes, we all do in the end." Spinks gave a dark little chuckle. "It's a coffin."

"Ah, yes, I see, sir. Very good."

Spinks ambled his way back after his meal, enjoying the rhythm of an easy, strolling gait. For a moment, he wondered what had made him make that silly riddle for the waiter. Another premonition?

It was all fixed for tomorrow, though, nothing to worry about. He would soon be very, very rich. Mad Sunday, then Happy Monday. He smiled and sang the lines of a song to himself. *As I walk along the Bois de Bologne with an independent air. Hear the girls declare: he must be a millionaire!* What was the rest? He couldn't remember. No, now he had to concentrate.

Because he had found himself lost in a maze of side streets, struggling to remember the directions back to the hotel. He had drunk a little too much wine for lunchtime; he would have to watch that. And he suddenly felt a pang of indigestion, and a growing sense of unease.

Where was he? he wondered desperately, all at once lost and disorientated. And it was then that a terrible sense of foreboding took hold of him. He was being followed; all of his long experience in surveillance and counter-surveillance alerted him to this fact. But now those well-

earned skills seemed useless in the proper evasion of the
threat. Every time he looked back, his shadow seemed to
have disappeared. But they were there, he was sure of it,
stalking him relentlessly.

He found himself walking toward the main route of the
road race. A motley array of motorcycles screamed by with
a furious insistence. The sound sickened in his stomach. At
speed, machine and rider became a single mythical creature.
Like centaurs caught between two natures, they seemed
harbingers of doom. Infernal engines that now displayed a
darker purpose, of accelerated destiny. Spinks felt himself
hurtling towards some awful providence.

He joined the throng of spectators, working his way into
the heart of the unruly congregation. To lose himself in the
crowd, he thought. But he was already lost. As he edged
closer to the racetrack, he realised, too late, that this was
precisely the wrong strategy to take. And as he made to turn
back, he felt a hand laid softly on his shoulder, a hard object
pressed into his gut.

"You know what this is," a voice hissed in his ear. "So
don't fuck about."

19

It was by the third day of her abduction that Jo became convinced that Chris Ipsworth was crazy enough to kill her. She had fought hard to keep her growing fear in check, to hold onto a vestige of self-control, but she could no longer deny the fact that he was ready to do something very foolish. That she would very likely be the victim of his sheer stupidity. He was fucking up badly again, and this made him really dangerous. All the carefully laid plans of a kidnap and a ransom demand were deteriorating into a messy act of warped revenge. And there was a horrible logic to this eventuality, she reasoned, even as she struggled in her mind to formulate an alternative. He had, after all, been well and truly fucked over by her husband.

They had blindfolded her in the back of the fake unmarked police car and driven her away in a deliberately erratic manner, constantly making sharp U-turns to disorientate her and scramble her sense of direction. Eventually, they were on an uneven road, some sort of country lane; she heard branches scraping against the bodywork. A dog barked in the distance as they pulled up.

As they dragged her out of the car, she caught the sickly-sweet smell of animal waste, the anguished drone of incarcerated livestock. With a man on each arm, she was led to a static caravan. She felt plastic sheeting under her feet as she was hustled inside. Still with her blindfold on, they made her strip off her clothes and change into a boiler suit and trainers. Then she was handcuffed and sat at a fixed table.

"Right, Jo," came Ipsworth's voice. "We need to get down to business."

"You are fucking dead for this!" she spat the words out at him.

It was the shock of the slap, as much as its force when it came, that knocked her out of her chair. A pair of hands roughly pulled her back into a sitting position.

"Watch your lip, bitch," Ipsworth told her. "Lee's not around to protect you anymore. He's... he's dead."

The note of triumph intended in this statement was blunted by the uncertainty with which it was uttered. Jo frowned. What was going through Chris's mind? He seemed ruffled somehow.

"Listen," he went on. "Hear that?"

Jo tuned in to the low grunting she could hear beyond.

"We're at a pig farm. We could kill you and feed you to them. They leave nothing behind."

She kept quiet and let the threat hang in the air.

"You don't think I'd do it?" he demanded. "Doesn't matter if I get caught for murder or kidnap, with my form. I've got nothing to lose."

And those words were the first daunting indication of how desperate he really was. Worse than that, he didn't seem to have thought any of this through.

"What do you want, Chris?" she asked, as softly and calmly as she could muster.

"You know what I want, bitch. I want what's mine."

He meant his share of the Tunbridge Wells Job, of course. But already, he seemed to have lost control of the situation. As ever the game villain, he had planned everything so well up to a point. Just as he had with the heist all those years back. He'd even used the same modus operandi, the fake unmarked police car to take her hostage, just as he had used for the tiger kidnapping of the depot manager. But just as with the robbery, once he'd got the prize, he clearly didn't know quite what to do with it.

"With Lee gone, it's going to be hard getting what's due to you," she reasoned. "Isn't it?"

"Yeah," he muttered thoughtfully, as if this was some deep conundrum. "Yeah."

"Look, we both wanted him dead," she reasoned, hoping to find some common ground between them.

"Did we, now?"

"Yeah. Did you kill him, Chris?"

Ipsworth laughed bitterly.

"No, I didn't. Did you?"

Jo wondered why he had left it too late, to kidnap her now, after Lee's death. He should have made a move before. Then a spark of something flashed through her brain. Maybe the fact of Lee's death had given him the power to act. But what could that mean?

"I want my fucking money!" he suddenly shouted, rousing her mind from this line of thought.

"OK," she tried to placate him. "OK. We'll talk to Craig, OK?"

Ipsworth grunted and stormed out of the caravan. Jo knew that she was playing for time; Craig wasn't going to be much use in a situation like this. They made a video of her later and sent it to him using the phone encryption system that Lee's syndicate used. "They're not fucking around, Craig," she spoke directly to the camera. "Do what they say, please. And don't go to the police." A text was added telling him to **wait for instructions**. Then they put the blindfold back on.

Although she couldn't see them, she could tell that there was always at least one person watching over her at any given time. And they always spent a lot of time carefully cleaning everything around the space they inhabited. This diligence in erasing any forensic trace became increasingly unnerving. Jo worked hard to keep a brave front. She would show compliance, she decided, but not fear. Though, in truth, she wasn't sure how long she could keep this up.

They brought her tea and stale sandwiches. A bowl of tepid soup. The smell of it nearly made her retch, but she forced herself to eat. To keep her strength up. She tried a set of breathing exercises she had learnt in a yoga class. There were times when she reached a kind of meditative state. And others when she felt a sickening panic rise up from the very core of her being.

At night, when they led her to a bed, she insisted that she would rather sit up in her chair with a pillow and a blanket. She didn't want to lie down, to appear that vulnerable in front of them. And she knew that she would get precious little sleep anyway. Instead, she would keep thinking, keep her senses about her.

And it was at night that she began to work out a plan in her mind. She soon came up with an idea, of something she could offer Chris, but she knew that she would have to be very clever about how she might go about it. If only she could gain his trust somehow, find his soft spot. It was there somewhere, she was sure of it, a weakness. Something to do with the hold that her late husband had once had over him.

And this was common ground between them, after all. They had both been so badly treated by Lee. It didn't take her long to consider the worst thing that man had done to her. Maybe if she told Chris about this, it might make him open up. Then they might find some kind of agreement. She just had to choose the right moment.

She found it hard to keep track of time, but she was pretty sure it was Saturday when Ipsworth really began to lose it. She could hear him in the next room of the caravan having an increasingly angry exchange with Craig. He ended the call and stormed through the trailer in a fury.

"Maybe we should cut off one of your fingers and send it to him!" he barked at her. "Then your stupid brother might realise that we're serious."

Jo thought it best not to respond to this and ducked her head submissively when she felt him nearby. She had to bide her time.

It was the following day when she made her move. A wet Sunday afternoon with a dull static tension in the air. The white noise of rainfall on a metal roof.

"Chris," she whispered so that he would come up close. "Take the blindfold off. I know what you look like, after all."

"I don't think so."

"Please. Send the others away. We need to talk. Face to face."

He made no reply. After about half a minute, he let out a sigh. There was movement elsewhere in the room as he muttered for the other two men to leave. When the caravan door clicked shut, he leant forward and pulled off her blindfold.

"Right, what is it?" he demanded brusquely.

"We need to sort this out."

"Then stop fucking me around."

"Look, Chris," she implored. "With Lee gone, and now Brian Colby dead, it isn't going to be easy getting what you want. But I think I know a way."

"Good. Because I'm getting my own back one way or another."

"OK. OK."

Jo felt her body clench up. She let out a breath slowly and carried on.

"You were set up. Lee fucked you over."

"Tell me about it."

"He was a right bastard. I know that."

"You have no fucking idea, bitch."

"Why did he treat you so badly?"

"Because I let him," Chris moaned, in mournful bitterness.

"What?"

"Never mind."

Those blue eyes were burning now, she was getting close to something, she was sure of it.

"What really happened between you and Lee?" she demanded starkly.

She watched him flinch at this. A raw nerve touched. For a moment, a terrible grief passed across his face like a shadow. Then his face was stern once more. Eyes cold.

"OK," he said, picking up the blindfold. "End of chat."

"Wait," she begged as he went to cover her eyes once more.

"I've had enough of this. It is getting us nowhere."

"Wait," she repeated.

This was the moment, she realised. The moment to make her confession. To let Chris know what Lee had made her do all those years ago. But she knew it wasn't going to be easy.

"Do you want to know what he did to me?" she asked softly.

He frowned and lowered his hands from her face.

"Go on."

20

"What do you want?" Spinks pleaded, obscenely pressed against his assailant by the scrum of bodies that surrounded them.

"You know what I want."

"It's in my hotel room."

The man frisked him, taking out his wallet and the hotel key card. Spinks thought about the sense of premonition he had had. And he recalled what Terry had said about fate with a dreadful sense of remorse.

"How did you know to come here?" he asked.

"I solved your riddle. Brian Colby left a clue."

"Who are you?"

Eddie smiled to himself. They were at the very edge of the racetrack now. Further down the road was a small grandstand, a red flag flapping in its forecourt, emblazoned with the symbol of the small province he had found himself in. He smiled at the three legs arranged in a wheeling triskelion. The man with three legs.

Three days before, in his own flat, he had found the part of the book that the lawyer's cold finger had pointed at. He had stared at it for some time, waiting for the cocaine to enhance the neurotransmission in the synapses of his brain. The page was headed: "Meditation XVII" and it was some sort of essay – about church bells ringing, reminding us how we are all joined through birth and death. Bells toll for the baptism of a child, for the burial of a man.

He came to the line that the lawyer had marked. *No man is an island, entire of itself*, it began. Yes, he knew that one. And how this long sentence ended: *for whom the bell tolls; it tolls for thee*. He had seen some book with that title at school.

Then it leapt out of the page at him. What Brian Colby had done with the single stroke of his pen. So simple. So fucking brilliant. It was a comma. A little dot with a tail. That protean spermatozoa that can conceive an entirely new meaning for a phrase.

No, man is an island.

Terry had mentioned Crown Dependencies when they'd first met at L'Escargot. The Isle of Man was one of them. *Man is an island*. That was the answer to Spinks's riddle. Man: an offshore tax haven, and home to the most dangerous motorcycle race in the world.

He had phoned Terry that night; they'd met the following day and started to make plans. They had to act fast. But Terry figured that even if Spinks was already on his way to the island, to cash in the bearer shares, this was unlikely to be arranged until the beginning of the following week. So they had the weekend to ambush him. Right in the middle of the Isle of Man TT, the big motorcycle race festival.

Eddie had contacted Jamal and got him to source an untraceable car and a forged driver's licence for him. He'd then driven up to Liverpool on the Friday and got the ferry from there.

"We can do a deal," Spinks begged. "Who are you working for?"

"Jo Royle. What you took belongs to her."

"No. It was Lee's. And mine."

"Is that why you had him killed?"

"No!"

"Then who did?"

"I really think it was this road rage thing. Typical Lee. He always wanted to be a businessman, but he was always too much of a gangster. Always ready to get into a ruck over nothing. No fucking self-control. Like with that undercover cop."

"But you did kill Brian Colby, didn't you?"

"Look, let's be reasonable, we can come to some sort of arrangement. There's plenty to go around. We can all be happy."

"I don't think so."

At that moment, two machines crested the slight hill that inclined into the long, straight section of the course that led to where Spinks and his predator stood. A purple and silver Honda Fireblade, followed closely by a bright-red Ducati Panigale. A couple of over-zealous amateurs keen to show off in front of the raucous Mad Sunday crowd.

"Come on, this is business," Spinks implored. "It doesn't have to become some sort of blood feud. You're an intelligent man. You solved the riddle, after all."

As the track ahead seemed to open up, the second rider hit the throttle and pulled out to overtake the rider in front. But the road here was not nearly as wide as it looked, and as the pursuer edged forward, he found precious little room to manoeuvre. As he accelerated once more to pass on the outside, he got caught in the lead vehicle's slipstream. This gave a slight wobble to his trajectory, enough to cause his front wheel to clip the back wheel of the motorcycle ahead.

"Yeah," said Eddie absently, turning his attention to the sparring engines.

"How did you do that?"

Eddie watched as the Fireblade toppled over, dragging the biker for a while as it skidded sideways in a shower of sparks. The Ducati somersaulted over it, throwing its rider clear as it cartwheeled towards the crowd. There were shrill screams of panic as the heavy machine tumbled into a group of spectators; mayhem as the motorbikes that followed sought to dodge the carnage. The Fireblade had now caught fire and was careering out of control.

Spinks saw that his assailant was distracted. And as the mob around them scattered, he saw his chance, gritting his teeth in a mordant grin. He'd foreseen this very moment, he thought; now he must take advantage of his prophesy. He pulled free from Eddie and turned to strike him. But his blow was parried, and now he felt the cold metal thrust into his face.

The pistol discharged just as the Fireblade's petrol tank exploded. And in the chaos, no one noticed Ray Spinks being shot in the head at point blank range. One eyewitness did see his body fall onto the road into the path of a vintage 1949 Vincent Black Shadow. It's rider, a sixty-four-year-old Mad Sunday veteran, having successfully weaved around the crash site on his ancient machine, was surprised by a spectator seemingly collapsed in his path. He was admitted to Nobles Hospital with multiple abrasions and a dislocated shoulder. Spinks was declared dead on arrival.

Three people were killed and four seriously injured that afternoon. Once more, there would be questions asked and a debate in the media concerning the safety of the Isle of Man TT. But not until the next day, after a post-mortem, would it be revealed that one of the casualties had died from a bullet to the brain.

Eddie walked slowly away from the scene of the crime. He put the gun back in his jacket pocket and took out the key card, still in its cardboard wallet with the room number and hotel address on it.

21

"And you just did what he told you?"

Tears prickled her eyes as she remembered the pain of it all.

"I was young, Chris," she tried to explain, if only to herself. "I was all on my own."

"Yeah," he nodded, as if he got it. "Yeah."

Jo felt emotionally raw. It had been such a long time since she had talked about what had happened. She had hoped her disclosure might generate some empathy between them, but she couldn't tell as she watched his face.

"You know how persuasive Lee could be," she said.

Chris let out a sad little laugh. Then he sighed and shook his head slowly, as if thinking something through. He seemed to be closing up again, his features stern and impassive once more.

"Well, we both know what a bastard your husband was," he said briskly. "But, as I said, it's getting us nowhere."

He raised the blindfold to her eyes once more.

"Wait," she said, desperately fishing for something to keep the conversation going.

"What?" he huffed impatiently.

"You remember Flicks? In Dartford?" she changed tack. "Back in the day."

Chris held her gaze coldly, but there was a glint of memory in his sad blue eyes. And Jo didn't have to force a smile when her mind flashed back to when they had first known each other. She was seventeen and had just started going out with Lee. Chris was the new, young face on the firm. The mixed-race, mixed martial arts fighter who moved with an animal grace. He had that deadly combination of beauty and menace that could inspire fear and desire in equal measure.

"You busted some moves on the dancefloor back then," she went on. "All the girls fancied you. And all the boys showed respect. They were shit-scared."

He flared his nostrils and flattened his mouth in a slight sneer, as if to indicate that he wasn't buying it. But Jo knew that he wasn't immune to flattery. She'd never known a man who was.

"Remember that night when that poor kid spilt your drink? He literally pissed himself. I mean, you could see the stain on his trousers."

"That was a thousand years ago," Chris cut in sharply. "Before I did a fucking eighteen stretch. All my good times down the fucking drain. I just want what I'm owed."

"But you and Lee were so tight back then. What happened?"

Chris stared at her for a long time. For a moment it looked like he was going to tell her something really deep and dark. He took a mouthful of air. Then let it out.

"No," he said.

"What?"

"Nothing happened. He was just a complete bastard. End of story."

He picked up the blindfold again, and she knew then that she had to execute the second part of her plan. She had hoped to get Chris more on her side at first, but there was no time for that now.

"Hang on a minute," she said.

"Stop fucking me around."

"Look, I can get you out of this mess."

"What?"

"Well, you are in a mess, Chris, face it."

"You've got a fucking nerve."

"I mean it. I can pay you off."

"What?"

"It might not be all you're due. But it'll be enough to go on with. And you can get it straight away."

"What the fuck are you talking about?"

"Well, you know that Lee arranged to have the missing ten million or so disappear into some elaborate money-laundering scheme?"

"Yeah."

"And with him and all the paperwork gone, it's going to be bloody hard to find any of it. But not all of it went offshore."

"No?"

"No. He put some of it aside without anybody else knowing. Not even Ray Spinks. Rainy-day money, he called it. Just a million of it, but all ready cash, in twenties, stashed away safe and close to hand. Got the idea from some documentary about Colombian drug cartels."

"What are you talking about?"

"He *buried* it, Chris. One million."

"Fuck."

"Yeah. And I can show you where it is. But tell me" – still keen to know his own weak spot with her late husband – "what really did happen between you and Lee?"

22

Eddie slipped into Spinks's hotel room unnoticed. The bar and reception area were still crowded with revellers, and the only serious concern that afternoon was the growing rumour of a terrible accident out on the racetrack. In the room, he found the document he was looking for at the bottom of a carry-on suitcase by the bed. He made a call on the specially encrypted phone Terry had given him.

"I've got it," Eddie told them.

"What about Spinks?"

"He's been dealt with."

"Really? How?"

"I've killed him."

Terry let out a dark chuckle.

"Clever boy," they said.

"Maybe. But not clever enough to know what this is," Eddie replied, scanning the sheaf of paper in his hand. "Remind me what the fuck it is that I'm looking at."

"I explained what bearer shares are."

"Tell me again."

"Right." A sigh came over the line. "So, you've got a lot of bent money and you want to put it somewhere safe, somewhere that can't be linked to you. So you set up a company, offshore, but you don't put your name on it. None of the business that company does, not a single transaction, not a single penny deposited or withdrawn, can be traced back to you. Then, that company can start moving its assets around and your money starts to make more money. You can leave it for years, until the police and insurers get tired of looking for it. And the villains that missed out on their share figure that it's gone for good. It's all completely undetectable, yet still in your grasp. How is that possible?"

"Bearer shares."

"Exactly. If you are in possession of the company's bearer shares – in actual, physical possession of them, that is – then the day will come when you can go and cash them in. In person."

"Right."

"But in the meantime, the money plays hide and seek in a maze of connections. A corporation in the Bahamas might be run by a trust in Wyoming, with investments realised in the Turks & Caicos. So if they come looking for it, it's always somewhere else. As I said before, the laundering doesn't happen in any one jurisdiction but in the movement between them. All managed by professional nominees acting as company directors and corporate lawyers protected by attorney-client privilege. This is how the magic happens. The French have a word: *paradis fiscal* – it's probably just a mistranslation of tax haven as tax *heaven*, but it's bloody apt. Something ethereal about the whole offshore thing. Offshore? It's off-world, more like. Until you bring it back down to earth."

"How?"

"With the original bearer shares of the original company. No name, nothing traceable, just a document. All you have to do is actually possess that piece of paper and present it at the place where it all started. That's the entrance to our labyrinth."

"So what do we do now?"

"Well, first of all, you're going to need to read the document to me. You've found the way in, my clever boy. An old hacker like myself is going to start to find our way out."

When he had finished dictating the share document to Terry, Eddie went downstairs and calmly walked through the hotel lobby out into the June sunlight. *No man is an island*, he thought, *entire of itself*. A week ago, he would have thought otherwise. He'd felt a loner all his life, emotionally offshore. As the poem had put it, never "part of the main." Jo had changed all of that. Now he felt as if the whole world was opening up to him.

For the first time, he really thought about what he had done and how it made him feel. Killing a man had been easy. The only shock was that there was no shock. And no hesitation; that seemed to him to be the key to it all. He had a dim recollection of some earlier bloodshed, that forgotten dream from days before. Perhaps a race memory of that primal instinct, or, as he had thought then, a prophesy of his newly ruthless self. A reflex for survival now weaponised for his own ambitions.

He had become a murderer, but the thought of that did not disturb him. He only really cared about getting away with it. His mind fizzed with ideas, and he felt a visceral excitement at it all. He could see now how serial killers got addicted. But the act of killing wasn't the buzz for him. It was a means to an end, and he knew now that he could be completely cold-blooded about it. He was bad, but he wasn't one of those weird psychopaths. This was just part of the game.

He had solved the riddle, cracked the code, and not just the childish conundrum Spinks had posed. He had broken the spell once and for all. That suburban, middle-class programming that he had been raised with. An ethic that gave you just enough to feel that you had something to lose. Now death entered his ego, and he had everything to gain.

The following day, he would really make a killing, as they say in the world of high finance. Every bit as ruthless as the bloody deed he had enacted that afternoon. Terry had hacked into the company named on the bearer shares to find that that an extraordinary general meeting had been called for Monday morning on the island, to deal with the arrangements of a major shareholder named only as "Mr Brown." Eddie would make his claim with all the necessary documents, Terry would supply the details of where to transfer the assets. Now he would prove himself to Jo and carve out a kingdom for themselves with her as his queen. He felt the sudden urge to call her. He had remained incommunicado since he had last seen her, unsure of where he stood or whether to trust her at all. He now felt the sudden urge to tell her that everything was going to be all right.

23

They had been digging for just over an hour when a disturbing image conjured itself in Jo's mind: that the hole they had made now looked very much like an open grave.

Chris Ipsworth's heavies had worked in shifts. One working the spade whilst the other trained a Vz 61 Škorpian machine pistol on her. Ipsworth stood by the growing pile of earth, the butt of an automatic pistol visible in his waistband. He held up a heavy black Maglite torch, tracing its beam into the void below.

"How deep is this fucking thing buried?" he demanded.

"Not sure," she replied.

"Are you sure this is the right spot?"

Jo nodded. She had been very precise about directions. They were on a patch of land with a disused barn on it that Lee had bought when he'd had a local councillor in his pocket on the planning department. The idea was to get permission to build a luxury development until the councillor managed to lose an election, and since then it had lain fallow. She had told Chris that the money was to be found exactly fifty yards due South of an old oak tree in the front field. He agreed that Craig would meet them here and he would hand her over to him once the loot had been found.

She could just about make out Ipsworth's face in the near darkness. It seemed a grim mask, cold and empty. It had been over twenty-four hours since he had made his terrible confession to her in the caravan, of what had happened to him at the hands of Lee Royle. Now she was far from sure that she had done the right thing in getting him to talk.

"The worst thing about it…" he had begun, eyes darting about the caravan even though he knew that they were the only ones there and that there was no chance of them being overheard.

"No," he sighed. "I can't tell you that."

"What?"

"The worst thing. I mean, we both know how bad Lee was but, right from the start…"

He had such an expression of guilt and shame. Something unbearable. Something that she recognised.

"Go on," she urged him.

"He used to come round our house. Dad was a villain, see? At the jump-up, you know, lorry hijacks, and Lee, well, he was a big fence for all that back in the day. Also good at making deals with his friends on the South East Regional Crime Squad. But anyway, this time Dad had got to go away for a bit. A seven stretch for armed robbery, and Lee turned up with some money for Mum. Parked outside our shitty council flat in Eltham in a big flash motor. He clocked the way I looked at it and let me sit in it. I was what, ten? Never felt such luxury. The driver's seat was more comfortable than anything in my own fucking home. I remember the smell of the leather upholstery.

"I knew then I wanted some of that. Just being close to it gave me hope. Lee was someone I could look up to. You know how charming he could be."

"Yeah, I do."

"Handsome. Well-dressed. Confident. I'd never known my old man really. Lee was like a real role model for me, and well…" He shrugged.

"What?"

Chris shook his head.

"Anyway," he went on, "he turns up when I'd just turned fifteen in this beautiful new Jaguar XJS. Says he could give me a driving lesson on some waste ground up in Woolwich. I could already drive by then. I'd been twocking motors for a couple of years. Already getting into trouble. So I take the wheel in this disused lot and I'm showing off. You know, handbrake turns, power slides, I want to impress him. And he's being all encouraging, joking and that, saying what a great getaway driver I could be."

He took a sharp intake of breath. Let out a sigh.

"Then he tells me to park in this empty shell of a warehouse. And that's when it happened."

"What?"

"He starts touching me. And then…"

Chris trailed off and Jo frowned for a moment, trying to work out what he was saying.

"You mean?"

"Yeah," he nodded gravely. "He raped me."

"No."

"Yes. And I didn't do anything to stop him. That bastard knew what I was before I knew myself. But I didn't want it to be like that. I wanted…"

He swallowed and made a little sobbing sound.

"I wanted him to kiss me," he muttered softly, like a prayer. "But he didn't do that. He never did that. He just fucked me. But you know what the worst thing was?"

"What?"

"I loved him. I loved him, so I let him treat me like shit. I became his dirty little secret."

"Christ."

"And I was on the down low about myself, too. Eltham was an ugly white ghetto back then. BNP graffiti everywhere. There were two things people didn't like in our neighbourhood. And I was both of them. I never felt I belonged. Half-caste – that was the name for it back then. And it worked like that in so many ways. I mean, black people could be homophobic, but there was a lot of racism on the gay scene, too. I remember being with this white guy in a bar in Soho and a friend of his turns round and says to him, 'I never took you for a dinge-queen.' Dinge? That makes the N-word seem polite.

"So I kept myself to myself. And I toughened up. Started boxing. Lee would come and watch me fight in these bouts at York Hall or Repton Boys Club. Take me to some hotel afterwards. Then cage fighting started up. Mixed martial arts. I started getting into that at a competitive level. Could have gone somewhere with it. Meantime, Lee was setting me up with jobs. Armed robberies, running security on big coke deals. Said his connections with the Old Bill meant it would always be sweet. Of course, even then, we knew that sometimes he'd be handing over people to them as well as money.

"He starts seeing you, and suddenly he ain't paying much attention to me. Yeah, I remember seeing you at Flick's. I remember him kissing you on the lips, grabbing you on the arse then looking over at me, as if to say, 'Look what I got. I don't need you anymore.' I suspected then that he wanted rid of me. I just never thought he'd do it in such a cold-blooded way.

"Because I thought the Tunbridge Wells Job would be something that could set me up for life. And my last big chance to prove myself to him. So I walked into a fucking trap. Became the fall guy for the whole fucking thing. Lee fixed it so enough of the cash would be recovered to keep the Kent Police happy. And the gang was handed to them on a plate with me as the fucking ringleader. A criminal mastermind, the press calls me. *The Sun* had me down as the most dangerous man in Britain. So, I get eighteen. Long years of wishing my life away and all I can think about is Lee-fucking-Royle.

"I brooded on these elaborate fantasies of revenge, but you know what they say: it's a thin line between love and hate. And I walked that line every day. I still loved him; that was the worst thing. The worst fucking thing, Jo. And all my anger just turned in on myself. He still had this hold over me. Some sort of charm. I mean, he had a charmed life, didn't he? Kills a cop and gets to serve five out of seven. With a lovely little nest egg of ten million or so, thanks to yours truly. Meantime I'm rotting away in Category A.

"And even when I come out, there's nothing I can seem to do about it. Oh, I had all these plans, but it's like I'm paralysed. There's even a part of me that deep down hopes he'll get in touch. Fucking pathetic. When I heard he'd been killed, I cried like a baby. And I realised then I'd never get over him. Maybe if I'd killed him myself, I could have done, but someone comes along and robs me of the chance. But I want my own back, Jo. I want my own back."

His blue eyes blazed wildly about the trailer, and she feared then that getting him to open up like this was a mistake. A new rage was building within him now. Smouldering, ready to catch fire at any minute.

All through the next day, Chris had become increasingly sullen in spite of the promise she had made of the money Lee had hidden on the smallholding over by Leyton Cross. They had waited until nightfall to drive over there. The fact that they had kept her handcuffed and were heavily armed wasn't the scenario she had hoped for.

Having to watch him carefully and to gauge his reactions to anything she might say gave Jo precious little time to process the revelations he had made about her dead husband. Thoughts about this and so many other things that had happened to her in the last few days had to take a backseat as she was ever vigilant of the ticking time bomb that was Chris Ipsworth. And with every minute that passed, she knew she was in deeper trouble.

Because the story about the million pounds that Lee had buried was a lie. She had made it up to buy herself some time while she imagined that she might find some common cause with her captor. As she spied him stand sternly over the tomblike pit they were excavating, she knew the chances of getting him to reach some friendly agreement with her now seemed slim. And there would be stark consequences when he found out that she had been deceiving him.

There was some distant engine noise and headlights flared up by the gate in the field above them. Craig had arrived.

24

As they patted Craig down for weapons, Jo wondered briefly if he might be hiding something. Some trick up his sleeve that could help them get out of this mess. But she knew too well that her brother had never been great at taking the initiative. Years as Lee's right-hand man had made him excellent at following orders but robbed him of any skill he might have developed in making plans of his own. And she'd had no opportunity to explain the false premise that he was seemingly part of. She could only hope now that they might somehow find a way of bluffing it out together. The man who had been doing the digging finished frisking him.

"He's clean," he said.

"So," said Ipsworth, now aiming the torch at Craig's face. "What do you know about this fucking buried treasure?"

"I told you," Jo interjected. "Lee only ever told me about it."

"I wasn't talking to you. So keep your fucking mouth shut." Chris handed the torch to the man beside him, pulled out his pistol and held it to Craig's head. "I want to hear it from him."

"What?" Craig's voice warbled a little in fear.

"Come on, big brother. What do you think we're digging for out here?"

"I don't know."

Chris clipped him sharply on the side of the head with the gun.

"Not good enough. Now, get on your fucking knees."

Craig did what he was told.

"Tell me about the million pounds that's supposed to buried out here," Chris demanded.

"I don't know. I don't know anything."

"Because it seems like a bullshit story dreamt up by your bitch of a sister. To give me the fucking runaround. Nothing you can say that might help me out?"

"Please. I don't know."

"You keep saying that, Craig. And it's really beginning to piss me off." Chris cocked the pistol and pushed the barrel between Craig's eyes. "I just want to know the truth. Do you know the truth, Craig?"

"No. No, I don't."

"Well, that's a shame." He looked over at Jo. "Looks like I'm going to have to jog your sister's memory. Maybe if I shoot you, it might just give a little shock to the system. Hmm?"

"Please," Craig begged.

"Listen…" Jo began, but Chris cut her off.

"Because I'm tired of all this! I'm sick to death of it and I just want some fucking payback. I want some revenge on the Royles and the Cadmoors. On everyone that fucked me over for all these years. So I might as well start with you, Craig."

Jo instinctively moved toward her brother, now whimpering on the ground before her. The man with the machine pistol cocked its bolt and prodded its barrel at her. As he stepped up on the slope of dirt by the pit, some of the earth crumbled beneath his feet and spilled into the hole below.

For a moment, all seemed possessed by stillness and a unanimous silence. A dark cloud passed overhead in the indigo sky. There came a distant pulse of white noise from the main road, the harsh cry of a rook in the trees above. Then a distinct crack of someone moving around in the darkness beyond.

"What's that?" Chris hissed at the man at his feet. "Who's out there?"

"I came on my own," Craig replied. "I swear."

"Shine it out there," Chris beckoned to the man with the torch.

But as the beam strafed the field below, it presented a perfect target to an intruder. There was a shot, and the torchbearer fell back into the pit, blood blossoming on his forehead. The light now flared up at Chris Ipsworth, making his face glower madly.

"What the fuck?" he spluttered.

The man with the machine pistol turned away from Jo, his footing a little unsteady on uneven ground. A whole clump of earth collapsed, and as he began to totter, he reached out instinctively, taking one hand off his gun. Seeing her chance, Jo grabbed at the weapon with both hands and, raising her right leg, gave him a firm foot jab she had learnt in a kickboxing class. With an indignant yelp, he toppled into the hole.

She now cradled a compact mechanism of death in her hands. Her right fingers instinctively found the butt and the loop of the trigger guard, her left followed the curve of the magazine as she pointed the muzzle towards Chris Ipsworth.

He stared at her incredulously, his pistol still pointed down at Craig's head. The torchlight hollowed out his sunken features, making his face skull-like. He already looked like a ghost. A doomed spirit. As he raised his gun slowly, he bared his teeth in a grin, a snarl.

Jo pulled the trigger. The Škorpian was locked on full-automatic and let rip. A rapid burst of seven rounds lacerated Chris Ipsworth's upper body, and he was thrown back and out of the light. She struggled to catch her breath as she spun around to face the intruder gaining ground on her. The gun now felt familiar in her hands. She was ready to use it once more.

"Wait," came a voice in the darkness. "Jo."

She hesitated for a second as he stepped into the torchlight. It was Eddie, an automatic in his right hand.

"Fuck," she gasped.

"Yeah," he replied.

"What? How did you…?"

"I'll explain later. Come on, we've got to move fast."

It was then that he noticed the man trying to crawl out of the pit beside him. Eddie peered down and levelled his pistol at him.

"Please…" the man begged.

"Sorry," said Eddie, and shot him in the head.

Craig was now sobbing openly, rocking back and forth on his knees as if in some mournful prayer. Eddie leaned over and slapped him hard across the face.

"Get your shit together!" he ordered. "We've got work to do."

They carried Ipsworth's body down the track to where Eddie had parked the car he had driven back from the Isle of Man. As they put the body in the driver's seat, Eddie wiped down the pistol he had taken from Brian Colby's house and put it in the dead man's hand. Then they set fire to the vehicle and drove away in Craig's BMW.

25

Jo and Eddie spent a long time showering together. They had been very careful to get rid of any forensic evidence. They tried to wash away something more indelible. But they were bonded by blood now. Eddie could still see Jo's crazed expression as she turned from killing Chris Ipsworth to point the gun at him. She yet held the image of his cold face as he shot the man in the hole, begging for his life.

And for the first time, Jo sensed a real vulnerability about her body next to Eddie's. She was a mess of bruises and broken nails, with matted hair and puffy eyes. Her flesh felt loose and mottled, and she was harshly put in mind of the difference in their ages. That he would always be leaner and fitter than her. Younger and faster, full of momentum. She knew that time was against her; she only wished that she could just slow it down a little.

But as she stepped out of the wet room and grabbed a towel, he followed. He reached out to touch her.

"Wait," she said. "We've got to talk."

"Yeah."

"You didn't say what happened."

"Spinks is dead."

"What?"

"Yeah. I found him and I killed him."

"How?"

"Oh, I'll explain it all. It's quite a story. But I had to put it all together myself."

"What do you mean?

"I mean, you didn't tell me anything, did you? Just expected me to go along with your plans. You didn't trust me, did you?"

"I didn't want you to get too caught up in all of this."

"Didn't you? Well, I am now, aren't I? I worked it all out."

"Yes."

"Spinks is dead. Ipsworth is dead. There's no one to fear now, is there? Except..."

He turned away from her.

"Who?" she whispered.

"Us," he said. "You and me."

"Yeah," she agreed. "That's scary."

"Then we have to trust each other. You want to know what happened?"

She nodded, and he spoke of how he had solved Ray Spink's riddle and followed him to the Isle of Man. How he had killed the man and taken back the bearer bonds. He explained that Terry Rice had hacked into the offshore company so that Eddie was able to transfer the funds at an extraordinary general meeting. The blind genius was now channelling the money out to the Far East. Through a tech corporation in Hong Kong and a gambling syndicate in Macau, to bring it back clean.

"But how did you know what happened to me?" she asked him.

"I tried phoning, and when I couldn't get through, I got Terry to hack into Craig's mobile. I saw the video that bastard Ipsworth sent him. In the end, I just tracked your brother when he drove out for the meet. The whole thing should look like a gang-related execution gone wrong. I shot those two guys with the gun that was used on Brian Colby. And Ray Spinks. They'll find it on Ipsworth, in a car that was driven to the Isle of Man. The ferry company will have a record of it. So all the murders can be traced to one convenient and very dead suspect."

"Chris," she murmured, remembering the ghostly face of the man she had killed.

"Yeah." He touched her face gently. "Look, you not telling me things at first, about Ray Spinks and the hidden money, I understand that. You had to be careful. But…"

"What?"

"I don't know, I just feel that there's something else you're not telling me."

She thought about what Chris had told her about Lee. It was less of a shock than she might have imagined. Just another betrayal like so many others. And she wondered for a moment if it could somehow explain what he had made her do all those years ago.

"Jo?"

"What?"

Men, she suddenly thought, can you ever trust them completely? She wondered for a moment if she could tell Eddie what had happened between her and Lee. Not yet, she decided, not yet.

He reached out once more; his fingers lightly raking the outline of her breast, stroking her ribcage.

"Tell me."

And could she really trust Eddie? His palm was on her belly now, and she felt joy and fear in equal measure. If there was new life growing here, she would have to find a way. But she needed time.

"There's nothing," she told him. "Honestly."

His hand ran along to her back, and he pulled her to him. Kissing her softly on the lips, tracing his mouth over her chin, pressing his tongue against her throat. She groaned and clawed at his hips.

"No secrets," he murmured as he felt her breasts press against him.

"No secrets," she echoed, knowing that it was a lie.

26

An informal business meeting was held at Sevengates the following week. Jo, Eddie, Craig, and Terry Rice sat around the large table in the dining room, which furnished an improvised boardroom for this new syndicate. Jo made sure that she was sat at the head with her lover and her brother on either side of her.

Eddie looked calm and confidant, leaning back in his chair. Craig was hunched over a little, cowed in the presence of his former sidekick. Ever since his breakdown at Leyton Cross, he'd become sullen and withdrawn. Grudgingly deferential towards Eddie, warily accepting of his relationship with his sister. This is the way that men organise themselves, Jo reasoned. Heads or tails. Who was top or bottom could change with the flip of a coin. It was mostly about simple, physical power and the wielding of it. And Eddie had proved worthy of respect in that regard, just as Craig had lost it.

Terry Rice displayed an altogether more nuanced strategy. Adopting a supremely arch demeanour, they channelled a partly feminine energy to cleverly undercut that brute manner of their biological species. And with this Terry was already putting themself forward as this new organisation's *consiglieri*.

"Eddie has already been registered as a director of a start-up company I set up a while back," they told the room. "A little tech firm run by some clever geeks in Shoreditch, specialising in developing phone apps with accessibility features for visually impaired users – voice-activated programmes, text-readers, things like that. Stuff I've been using, and adapting, in my line of work for years now. And they've had some interesting results, applications that can be used for all sorts of functions. Anyway, in a few days' time, this enterprising little company is going to be bought out for millions by a Chinese investment firm."

Jo laughed.

"The money from the Isle of Man account," she said.

"Exactly," Terry went on. "So we have a legitimate audit trail. And you've got the funds to set up your own company."

"A partnership," Eddie said, looking over at Jo.

"I understand you plan to get married?" Terry asked.

"Yeah," Jo nodded.

"Excellent idea," Terry concurred. "If only for tax reasons."

"What?" Craig straightened up for a second.

"We were going to tell you," said Jo. "We want this to be a family business. To keep it tight."

"Right," Craig huffed, and looked across the table.

"We'll be brothers-in-law." Eddie forced a smile.

"And I'm sure we can all appreciate the irony," Terry continued. "But a legitimate front is going to be crucial. Not only to provide an honest conduit for funds acquired by, er, nefarious means. But we have the opportunity now to move into a really big racket."

"And what's that?" asked Jo.

"Information. Look, we agreed that we'd form some kind of IT firm, didn't we?"

"Yeah," said Eddie.

"Well, I'm suggesting we set up a private intelligence company."

"And what's that?" Jo asked.

"It will specialise in information analysis. Develop a state-of-the-art expertise in surveillance, counter-surveillance, encryption, and data acquisition. Then we can really expand in terms of demographics. Into strategic communication, opposition research, disinformation…"

"You're beginning to lose us, Terry," Jo warned them.

"Yes, quite. Well, let's maybe just see knowledge as a commodity. And that there's a really fast-growing black market in this product, just like drugs were back in the Eighties. But far more corrupting. I mean, narcotics simply fuck up the mind of the user. But information, that can completely control it. And with this intelligence, we can not only protect the security of all of our enterprises, but compromise that of our competitors. I mean, we know Lee was always informing on his rivals, right back from when he was tipping off the regional crime squad about lorry hijacks. Well, now…" They shrugged.

"We can grass them up on a technological level," offered Craig.

"Exactly! And Jo" – Terry turned to her – "this will give you the power to take control of all of Lee's former dealings and operations that we can feed into the new corporation."

"I've known his business from the inside," she declared. "He never gave me credit for it, but I was always there. I was privy to things that nobody else knows."

"And Eddie can be the perfect face for our new company," Terry continued. "The budding young entrepreneur. Not on the radar as a major player with any law enforcement agencies, as such. A bit of juvenile form, but we can do a PR job on that. A story of redemption, a bad boy made good. Perhaps we could set up a charitable foundation for the rehabilitation of young offenders," Terry suggested. "In the meantime, you both become influencers, as they say. And in so many ways. You two will be a real power couple."

Craig watched grudgingly as Jo and Eddie beamed at each other.

"What about me?" he asked quietly, his tone almost apologetic.

"Well," Jo began, suddenly conscious of how awkward her brother felt. "You'll still be running county lines, won't you?"

"Yeah," said Eddie. "And you can step up in that department, if you ask me. You know all the faces. They've still got your respect."

"But" – Craig shrugged – "I lost my bottle, didn't I?"

There was an awkward silence for a second, and Jo knew that she had to reassure her brother.

"Well, this is your chance to get it back," she said.

"And I can assure you all," Terry added, "as well as expecting a healthy income stream from this side of the business for many years to come, the particular talents of the manpower involved will continue to be a useful resource, if you know what I mean."

"Yeah," said Jo. "Having a bit of muscle to call on will always come in handy."

"So, we need you back in the game, mate," Eddie insisted.

"You're blood, after all." Jo reached out and patted his hand with her own. "In terms of trust, there's nothing as strong as that."

Eddie glanced over at them both and felt a brief but sharp pang of disquiet. Maybe he'd always be seen as an outsider, he thought, as he watched them share a moment. He turned away and caught sight of Terry Rice. That ancient face seemed to glow exultantly with empty eyes that saw everything.

"And, of course," they said. "Some of those more unruly elements might have to be persuaded that this new succession of power is in their best interests."

"Yeah, well," said Craig. "There's one thing we do have to, isn't there? Before we get this sorted."

"What's that?" asked Jo.

"We've got to bury Lee."

27

Lee Royle's funeral was a stately affair. A cortege of limousines filed into St John's Cemetery in Margate in solemnly measured procession. Filled with local faces and emissaries from fiefdoms as far off as Catford, Clerkenwell, Bermondsey, and Canning Town. Flanked on foot by a phalanx of thickset men in black, a solemn bodyguard of doormen and debt collectors, all come to pay their last respects. On top of the lead hearse lay a floral tribute, an epitaph picked out in white carnations: THE KING OF KENT. And the press pack that had hounded Royle's demise now huddled by the lychgate.

Jo scanned the crowd of stony-faced men as she stood by the graveside and noted something narcissistic about their kind of grief, as if it were just another excuse for power-dressing. We mourn ourselves, our own sense of mortality, she realised then. And she knew that she herself looked good in black, just as impressive as they were. She was determined to appear fierce as well as sombre on this day, looking each one of them in the eye as they proffered their hands and muttered their grandiose condolences. *If they only knew what Lee had really been like,* she thought to herself.

With Craig by her side, she presented that strong front of family and continuity. Strikingly regal, the grieving queen still holding the power of the throne. Eddie stayed in the background for now, as rumours buzzed of a new player in the kingdom, standing in the shadows.

For weeks now, news desks and crime reporters had eagerly fed on the story, of how the still-unsolved killing of a gangster had seemed to set off a tribal conflict, culminating in a bloody massacre in the badlands of Kent. The triple slaughter of Chris Ipsworth and his cohorts at Leyton Cross already threatened to become as much a part of home-grown gangland folklore as the Rettendon Range Rover murders.

And with a widening sense of conspiracy, this gruesome mythos was linked to the strange death of Commander Ray Spinks, now confirmed to have been killed by a bullet wound to the head. With its habitual instinct for obfuscation and reputation management, Scotland Yard loudly refused to either confirm or deny unofficial reports that this controversial detective had been murdered whilst engaged in a covert operation connected to the Tunbridge Wells Job. Ever the enigma, Spinks took his secrets to the grave.

Ipsworth had been found dead in possession of the murder weapon, in a car that had driven to the Isle of Man on the weekend of his killing, but there were so many anomalies that it did not seem possible that Chris had actually assassinated this senior police officer. What seemed more likely was that someone had arranged it to look like that. And that person was a force to be reckoned with. With Craig keeping the old syndicate in operation, this narrative would help to pave a way for Jo's succession, with this mysterious new face as her consort.

And it served to distract the public eye from more subtle machinations in the black economy. So *The Sun* was able to claim that their much-vaunted "most dangerous man in Britain" had met his end in a suitably tragic manner, when this was not much more than collateral damage in the greater scheme of things. Elsewhere, there was enough speculation as to some newly-ordered organised crime group to make any opposition cautious and ready to negotiate. Though, the fact remained that these supposed structures were far more pragmatic than most people imagine. Crime, like other forms of capitalism, thrives on chaos as much as organisation.

As they laid Lee Royle to rest, amid whispers of a ruthless new regime, the biggest myth of them all was once more trotted out. Of a lost era of codes and honour, of respect and tradition. That ancient lie of an old order (one that had never really existed) coming to an end.

As the congregation began to recede from the graveyard, Jo knew it was time for her to pay her last respects to Lee. Eddie waited by her side, but she waved him away.

"Give me a moment, babe," she told him.

Turning her back on the world to stare down into his tomb, she scooped a fistful of dirt. Even though she carried the legacy of their secret, she could make her peace with him now. Now she might bury it all for good, she could hope for that. She weighed the earth in her hand for a moment, then scattered it like seed that clattered on the coffin lid.

Two weeks later, a more private ceremony took place as Jo Royle and Eddie Pierce were married in a secluded country club in the Weald. Neither of Eddie's parents were present, as he had remained estranged from them. Jamal, his old friend from Feltham, acted as his best man.

And Craig took the father's role of giving Jo away, as their dad had walked out on their mother many years ago. Craig was quietly zealous in his actions to demonstrate the elevated status of the new member of the family. And one function of this wedding rite was to consecrate this new status quo in front of a select audience.

The congregation included many of Lee Royle's close business associates, as well as some of his erstwhile rivals. There were representatives from the syndicate that Eddie and Jamal had worked for. And strong incentives had been offered to secure their approval: they had all been made shareholders of a new venture. Theban Enterprises provided them with a respectable business profile and the technical resources to avoid unwelcome curiosity in any financial irregularities.

But there was some disquiet, particularly among the more old-school entrepreneurs that had plied a more vigorous trade with Lee Royle in the past, with many hard knocks along the way. They were rightly suspicious of Eddie. Who was this young chancer and where had he come from? For all his clever talk of securing a legitimate front for their activities, his own lineage was unknown, and his authority uncertain.

With keen senses as ever alertly psychic, Terry Rice picked up on this mood of indignation amongst the men in the room. These old lags imagined that they understood the order of things. It was time for an intervention.

Terry stood up and quelled the hubbub with the gentle tintinnabulation of dessertspoon against wine glass. In tightly tailored morning dress, hair scraped back from a buffed and lightly stubbled face, the blind seer looked strikingly epicene.

"Ladies and gentlemen," Terry began.

"And which are you today?" a gruff voice called from the back.

Undeterred by a burst of mocking laughter from the assembly, Terry scanned the room with those milky blue eyes that looked far beyond mere vision.

"Billy Mears." The heckler was identified coldly and now seemed transfixed by the sightless glare of the speaker. "Hmm. I know of some rather interesting photographs of you, taken in a hotel in Broadstairs. They rather prove that I'm as much a man as you'll ever be."

Some low howls of outrage ululated amid the crowd at this, but Terry sensed a dread quietening take hold of the men as they now gave their full attention. Terry knew their secrets, and, as Billy Mears dropped his head in shame, they were all alert to the possibility that they might be the next in line for this particular form of divination. This is what they most feared, that part of their nature that they themselves might never comprehend. What the tipster, the trickster, the consummate shapeshifter could expose.

"Oh, I know all about you," Terry drawled imperiously, reading their minds, hacking into their souls. "You think I'm the weirdo, but you lot are the bloody freak show. And you talk about tradition, but you don't even know where you come from. You call yourselves English? You need a fucking history lesson.

"So, let's raise a glass to the ancient Kingdom of Kent. The Garden of England. The oldest county, founded just after the Romans left. It's an interesting story. A gloomy monk called Gildas wrote the first account of it back in the sixth century. He called it *On the Ruin of Britain*, so, yes, pundits were droning on about how the country was going to hell in a handcart even back then.

"It was a time of change and uncertainty, a post-colonial society in decline, with a decaying imperialist infrastructure it could hardly maintain. A bit like now, I suppose. And barbarians were causing trouble all the time. The British leader back then, a man called Vortigern, well, he needed a bit of extra muscle. So, when a young face called Hengist turned up from across the sea, team-handed with a crew of lively hooligans, he thought his troubles were over. They were offering a bit of extra security, you know, protection. Well, I don't need to tell you lot how that went, do I? This Vortigern was a bit of a soft touch, and soon enough Hengist had taken over the whole manor of Kent for himself.

"Gildas writes about how foolish Vortigern was, that employing Hengist was like inviting 'wolves into the sheepfold.' So, think about our history and ask yourself: which are you? A wolf or a sheep? Because, back then, while the sheep moaned on about something coming to an end, it was the wolves that knew that this was a new beginning. This was the beginning of England. A stab in the back, the double cross: that's our tradition, gentlemen. And I defy anyone here to tell me any different. So why not be proud of it?"

There were grim murmurs of assent at this.

"'Hengist' is Old English for male horse or stallion, and also the root for the word henchman. He was a hard man, a heavy, 'staunch' as some of you used to say. 'Hench', as the younger generation have it. But a clever racketeer, too. We call his time the Dark Ages, but he simply saw it as a time of opportunity. Like us, he belonged to the kleptocracy. So, he took Kent from Vortigern and became its king by force and by cunning. And he went from being a chancer from nowhere to a legitimate ruler, just like that."

Terry Rice clicked their fingers.

"This is our lineage, my friends; we take advantage of the dark times. And we take what we want. Or stand by someone bold enough to take it. And this is where we come from. We're strangers, interlopers, economic migrants from Northern Europe that went on to become the English. Hengist was just the first of them. It's a tradition that belongs to the future as much as to the past.

"So don't think that there's no precedent for Kent being up for grabs. It's always been a gangster's paradise. It might the Garden of England, but it's the tempting serpent that really knows how to exploit it. You all have an opportunity here to be at the start of something really big. So here's to the kingdom of Kent." Terry raised a glass and tipped it towards the couple sat at the top table.

"And a queen and king worthy of it. To Jo and Eddie."

As the room echoed this salutation, Terry nodded to where they knew the stage to be, to signal for the wedding band to start the first number. And the newly married couple took to the floor to begin a stately slow dance.

"You've hardly touched the champagne," Eddie murmured to Jo when they found a quiet moment together later that afternoon.

"I'm happy enough. I don't need a drink."

"Really?" he said, noting that her smile seemed a little forced.

"Yeah." She reached out to touch him, to reassure him.

"Maybe there's another reason that you're off the booze."

"What do you mean?"

"Come on, Jo, I've heard you puking your guts up in the bathroom every morning this week. And don't say it was wedding nerves."

"No."

"You're pregnant, aren't you?"

She sighed.

"I meant to tell you."

"Then why didn't you?"

"Well..." Jo shrugged, casting around her mind for an excuse. "All this talk about making things legitimate, I just wanted that for our child."

"That's bullshit. I thought we said: no secrets."

"Yeah but..."

"What?"

"I just wanted to be sure," she murmured.

"Even so."

His stony eyes glared at her, searching for the truth, and suddenly finding fear.

"What?" he quizzed her once more. "You wanted to be sure of me?"

She shrugged.

"Christ, Jo," his expression softened, his eyes widening. "This is just what I want. Don't you realise?"

"I guess."

There was a stupid, infectious grin on his face now. She could see the happy child in him, and that gave her hope. At that moment, she knew that she could trust him. Whether she could trust herself, well, that was another matter.

But she beamed a bright and honest smile back at him, caught up in the delight of it all, able to forget the dread beneath. He laughed.

"Everything's going to be all right," he said, touching her belly. "That's what this is all about, right? You said it yourself. Blood. Family."

She stroked his face gently and felt a genuine sense of relief. It was true that she wanted to be absolutely certain about how he felt in regard to them having a child together. And this seemed settled at least. But with this almost ecstatic sense of fulfilment came a terrible fear. She thought she had buried her secret with Lee, yet it still haunted her. Eddie took her in his arms and, possessed by a precarious joy, she gave in to the embrace. She knew that she had never been so happy in her life. Nor so scared.

PART II

28

It was the sound of the baby crying that woke him from his nightmare. Eddie came to with a start, his daughter's wailing like an echo of some primal scream in his own consciousness. Jo stirred beside him, roused as much by his sudden awakening as the sound of Annie howling in the next room.

"It's OK," Eddie whispered to her. "I'll go."

The bad dreams and the headaches had begun soon after their first wedding anniversary, after that visit from Kent Police informing them that the murder investigation was being wound down. At night came visions of violence and terror. By day, blinding migraines would rack his mind.

He carefully picked up Annie from her cot, scooping her up in his arms to cradle against his chest. Eddie hushed her softly, finding some soothing comfort of his own as he rocked their bodies together in a slow rhythm. Her mewling subsided, a minor tragedy fading into the dawn.

He weighed the heft of her. They grew so quickly, he thought. Annie would soon be crawling, walking on all fours through the riddle of life. He sighed as a strange truth entered his brain once more: that he felt more helpless than she was.

Jo came through and reached out for her child.

"Careful," Eddie said as he passed her over. "She's just dropped off."

"Right," Jo murmured as she took Annie and went to put her back in the cot.

"I'll think she'll sleep now," she told Eddie. "Come back to bed."

"No. I'm going to get up."

"What's the matter?"

"Nothing."

"You've not been sleeping well."

"No."

"The nightmares again?"

"Yeah."

"What are they about?"

"Mmm."

His face froze. Jo reached out to touch him.

"Eddie?"

"Murder," he blurted the word out.

"What?"

"I dream of murder, Jo. Of the people I killed."

He glared at her. Jo's eyes widened back at his.

"We've both killed people, Eddie," she said with an edge to her voice she hadn't quite expected. "We've got to live with that."

"Yeah," he replied in a tone as flat as hers. "But there's something else."

"What?"

"Another murder."

"What do you mean?"

"Lee."

"Oh, Christ, Eddie," she sighed. "Not that again."

"It's like we're cursed."

"Please."

"I mean it, Jo. I don't think I'll rest properly until we find out who killed him."

Later that morning, she came downstairs to find him fully dressed in the kitchen.

"I'm going out," he told her.

"What?"

"I've got to get out. Some things I need to check on."

"Like what?"

"The Folkestone consignment."

A major cocaine importation from Amsterdam was being arranged to come through that port in flower trucks.

"But that's Craig's job, isn't it?" Jo insisted.

"Yeah, well…"

"I thought we decided my brother would deal with that end of the business. He won't appreciate you checking up on him, will he?"

"We need to keep an eye on things. We need to keep an eye on everything."

"Look, Terry Rice is coming by today, remember? With this big new plan of his. *That's* what you should be concentrating on."

"Tell him I'll see him at the London office tomorrow."

"Eddie," Jo called after him.

But he was already making his way out of the door.

Jo struggled to keep her exasperation from turning into a sense of real dread and foreboding. She had just crawled out of her own pit of despondency. The post-partum depression had been so bloody awful. And just as she had begun to put it behind her, Eddie was now descending into his own dark place. She feared being dragged down by his obsession with Lee's murder, back down into the grim memories of her dead husband and what he had made her do all those years ago.

Determined to keep in a positive frame of mind, she spent some time playing with her baby daughter that morning. Annie was in a good mood; this seemed a golden age of her babyhood. The child had developed a much more discernible personality now, mimicking facial expressions and becoming so much more expansive and responsive. An easy audience and an eager performer. It was in these moments that Jo felt blessed with a sudden happiness. She was beginning to be sure she was over the worst of it.

And this gave her the courage to think about how she might actually deal with her past. To turn and face it somehow, rather than let its shadow darken her life. A plan began to form in her mind that might also resolve Eddie's preoccupations. Something that might help him deal with his demons, and maybe solve the mystery of her own terrible secret.

Terry Rice arrived just after eleven in a chauffeur-driven Mercedes, and Jo went out to greet him by the fountain. He wore a cream linen suit with an open-necked silk shirt. A Malacca cane tapped at the gravel drive as he climbed out of the back of the car. She came forward and took his arm.

"Terry, you're looking well."

"The miracles of medical science," he smiled. "Worth every penny."

"Eddie's not here, I'm afraid," she explained.

"Fine." He put his hand over hers. "That will give us some time to ourselves."

It was a bright, warm day, so they went into the garden. Fraser, the Doberman, followed them out then bounded away to claim the liberty of Sevengates. Terry took hold of Jo's elbow lightly, and she led him through to the orchard, weaving their way through the trees.

"Ah," he sniffed the air, catching the scent of the apples. "Flower of Kent, unmistakable. The very same variety Isaac Newton observed falling to the ground."

"You're having me on," she retorted.

"Look it up, dear. Look it up."

"Well, even this beautiful place was something of a front for Lee, you know? When he had that bloody thing built." She gestured to the hangar-like outhouse that loomed beyond.

"What thing?"

"Sorry, you're actually lucky you can't see it. It's a big drive-in shed. Ugly thing. When Lee asked for planning permission, he claimed it was an apple store. For his orchard."

"So he had these apple trees planted? That was very thoughtful of him."

"Yeah. It all provided good cover for loading or unloading lorries. Especially the ones that had been hijacked."

"Quite."

"So, what's this big idea of yours, Terry?"

"Heh, heh," he made a little chuckle. "You don't hang about, darling."

"No, I don't. So come on, then."

"Well, as you know, we've been successful in feeding information about our rivals to various agencies. A bit here a bit there, you know? There's Border Force and the National Crime Agency. We've got the Met's Serious and Organised Crime Command, as well, and even our own Kent Police's County Lines and Gangs Team. We can even play them against each other, but it's all been a bit piecemeal. It would be good to coordinate it all a bit."

"What are you suggesting?"

"That we move up the food chain. Become an asset for the Security Services."

"You're kidding."

"I'm entirely serious. This could give us real protection. And you'd be surprised at how keen the charmingly named 'intelligence community' are to get their hands on what we can offer them."

"Really?"

"Really. But we need to give them something. To prove we mean business."

"And what would that be?"

"Well, you know that for organised crime – and espionage, for that matter – counter-surveillance is always the thing, particularly in terms of communication. Encrypted phones, that's the big thing now, and everyone's looking for the most watertight system. We're in the position of developing something that we could market through our own networks in the underworld, through word-of-mouth recommendations and on the dark web. A device that can offer the most secure messaging service in the world. We have the technology, after all, and the significant contacts with all the major criminal operators."

"You mean we develop our own encrypted phone system and sell it to other syndicates?"

"Exactly. And once we've established its credibility, well, then we can offer complete access to it to our friends in MI5. In exchange for something of a free hand in our own activities."

"That's brilliant. Will it work?"

"I think so, yes. And if it does, it could make you virtually untouchable."

"You're a clever bastard, Terry Rice."

"I do have a certain foresight, yes."

"Is there anything you don't know?"

"Knowing things isn't the answer to everything, Jo. A gift can be a curse," he muttered darkly.

"What?"

"Never mind," he went on, wanting to change the subject.

"Never mind my mind. What about my corporeal self?"

"Sorry?"

"My body. What do you think of the new me?"

"I already said, you look great. You're a man again, and a handsome one at that. So, you've completely de-transitioned?"

"*Re*-transitioned, I prefer to call it. Yes, but look, I'm still trans. That's what a lot of people don't get. I'm not in any kind of denial of what I went through in the past. I'm the ultimate trans person. A completely transitional identity. Not for the faint-hearted though. Lots of reconstructive surgery, of course. Cost a fortune, too. But it's the emotional changes that are the most important. Life is a strange journey."

"You're telling me."

"So." He narrowed his sightless gaze at her. "How's yours?"

"My life?" she smiled. "I'm feeling good, Terry."

"I understand things weren't entirely easy for you after the birth."

"Hmm, yeah, you know." She shrugged. "The baby blues."

"People can make light of these things, Jo. I know how serious they can be."

"I'm through the worst of it, Terry. Honestly."

"But something is troubling you. I can tell."

"It's Eddie," she sighed. "He's having a hard time. I think the stress of it all is getting to him. But he can't leave anything alone. He was supposed to be here today, but instead he's chasing up a big consignment from over the water."

"I thought Craig was dealing with that side of things."

"He is, but Eddie likes to throw his weight around. And he doesn't trust anyone. I think all this power has made him paranoid."

"An occupational hazard, I'm afraid."

"And he's got obsessed with Lee's murder, just as they're winding down the investigation."

"Oh, dear." Terry frowned. "Why?"

"I don't know; it's like all of a sudden, he's identifying with him."

"Hmm, that's interesting."

"Thing is, I'm worried that he's becoming like Lee. And I really don't want that to happen."

29

"The good news is that the MRI scan is clear," said Doctor Ibrahim Hakim.

Eddie was sitting in the panelled consulting room of a large Georgian house in Harley Street. He had come here in secret the week before for a series of tests. He didn't like lying to Jo, but if it was something serious, he wanted to protect her from the truth of it for as long as possible.

"There's no sign of a tumour, or lesions," the neurologist went on. "No inflammation or bleeding; no damage from injury or a stroke. No. You have a very healthy brain, Mr Pierce."

"So why am I getting these terrible headaches?" Eddie asked him.

"Well" – Doctor Hakim shrugged – "the fact is, we don't know. These things are not yet fully understood. For most primary headaches there is no visible cause. We simply don't know where they come from."

"You mean, you don't know what they are?"

Eddie's gaze strayed to the palm plant in a glazed pot in the corner of the office. He had tried to prepare himself for some dread discovery. Some terrible but certain fate. Instead, he faced the unknown once more.

"We can make a diagnosis, Mr Pierce. From your symptoms and your history. And don't worry, I'm certain that we can find a suitable treatment for this problem."

"God, I hope so."

He looked back at the doctor. Then down at the desk in front of him.

"But it's important that we look at associated factors and what might be triggering these episodes," the doctor went on. "I'm concerned about these nightmares you mentioned."

"Really?" Eddie frowned.

There was a stethoscope curled up on the desk. The long, thin hammer Doctor Hakim had used to test his reflexes next to it.

"Yes, there is a possibility that these headaches have some psychological cause. You might want to consider that."

"What do you mean?"

"Anxiety or stress can create extreme symptoms," he explained. "As can trauma."

"Trauma?"

"Yes. The brain is under tremendous pressure when dealing with traumatic events. And painful or difficult memories often become severely repressed."

"Repressed?"

"Look," Doctor Hakim sighed. "I'm no expert in this field, Mr Pierce. I deal with the more mechanistic aspects of brain function. But it might be worth exploring the possible psychological aspects to your problem. And I can certainly refer you to someone that might help you with this."

After the appointment, Eddie walked to his car with a prescription for specialised painkillers and the business card of a consultant psychotherapist.

The talking cure; that's what Doctor Hakim was suggesting. How could that work? Eddie wondered with grim disdain. A confidential heart-to-heart on how he had murdered men in cold blood? No, that wasn't going to happen. And he had no time for guessing games. He wanted simple answers. Facts. Knowledge.

He drove out to meet Jamal at a lock-up on a run-down industrial estate by the river in Dartford.

"You wanted to talk about the Folkstone thing?" he asked Eddie, as he pulled up the metal shutter.

"Never mind that. There's something else."

"What?"

"I want you close, Jamal." Eddie looked around at the concrete forecourt. "You're the only one I can really trust. We go back before any of this happened."

"Before what happened?"

"Lee Royle's murder. I need to find out who did it."

"Right." Jamal nodded slowly, hesitantly.

"They think they got away with it, and I can't let that happen. They'll be after me next."

"Er, OK. So, what do you want me to do, bruv?"

"Let everybody know. I want this guy. Someone has to give him up. Spread the word."

"Sure."

"And I'm willing to pay well for any information."

"I get you."

"If anybody knows anything I want them to come to me. But let them all understand this: I'm going to find this person even if it means turning the whole of Kent upside-down. The police have given up on it. It's up to us now."

"Yeah?"

"Trust me. I want this dealt with in-house. If anybody is hiding them or knows anything and is keeping it to themselves, then they better watch out. Because I'm going to come down on them as well."

"Have you talked to Craig about this?"

"That's another thing. You take your orders directly from me from now on, OK? And as for Craig, I want him followed."

"Followed?"

"You heard me. Round the clock. Call in some extra talent if you need it, but I want you to keep an eye on him for me."

It was late afternoon by the time Eddie got back to Sevengates. Jo was on the sofa in the living room with Annie in her Moses basket on the floor.

"Hello," he said softly, leaning over to kiss her on the cheek. "You OK?"

"Yeah." He sighed and went over to where the baby was lying.

"Hey!" Eddie crouched down and made a wide-open face. He watched delightedly as his daughter mimicked his expression. "Hello!"

Annie let out a gurgling laugh as he tickled her belly. Jo noted how much pleasure playing with Annie gave Eddie. And it calmed him down so. But she also knew that their child needed her rest, too.

"Go easy with her," she told him. "She's just getting off for her afternoon nap."

"Right," he said.

He collapsed on the couch and rested his arm on the seat behind her.

"So," she kissed him. "The old bugger's come up with something really special."

Jo explained Terry Rice's plans to approach the security services. And his idea to develop an encrypted mobile phone and what they could do with it.

"He's a clever bastard," Eddie said when she had finished.

"That's what I said to him. You know, I kind of believe this bollocks he talks about."

"What do you mean?"

"You know, about being clairvoyant."

"Yeah." Eddie sat up and nodded thoughtfully.

"He's certainly got something, that's for sure," Jo went on.

"He knew about Lee and Ray Spinks, of course."

"What? Yeah, well, Spinks used him as a phone hacker, didn't he?"

"Until Terry double-crossed him and came to work for us. Maybe..." Eddie stood up suddenly. Annie made a little squeal.

"Careful," said Jo. "She was just getting to sleep."

Eddie went over and crouched down once more, rocking the basket gently.

"Shh," he hushed.

"What were you saying?" Jo asked him.

"Doesn't matter," he replied in a whisper.

30

An aura: that's what Doctor Hakim told him it was called. The signs of an oncoming headache: flashes in his eyes, pins and needles in his face. He stood up from his desk and walked to the broad, landscape window of his office. Thirty-three floors up, Theban Enterprises had acquired an impressive London headquarters. Eddie looked down and tried to relax his mind.

Perhaps he was repressing something, but drug therapy seemed the best course of treatment for now. He reached into his pocket to find the small bottle and pulled it out. "ALMOTRYPTAN 12.5 mg" read the label. Perhaps the correct medication might stop the bad thoughts that were infecting his brain. He unscrewed the lid, shook out a pill and swallowed it dry.

Sasha, his personal assistant was at the door.

"Terry Rice is here," she said.

"Good," said Eddie. "Show him up."

He scanned the skyline as he waited. A cluster of monstrous towers now subjugated the meagre square-mile plot of the old city. Colossal and grotesque forms that seemed not merely temples of greed, but the effigies of false gods. Forcing all below to bow in worship. A pantheon of graven idols in glass and steel. Built and sustained by all the plundered loot of the world.

"Here he is," came Terry's rich voice as he entered.

He was looking elegant in a pearl-grey Prince of Wales check suit and mirrored Ray-Ban's. A silver-topped cane in his right hand. Eddie came forward and they embraced gently.

"Terry." Eddie said the name softly, affectionately. "It's good to see you. We've missed you around here."

"And I'm keen to get back to work. There's life in the old dog yet."

"Jo told me about your plan. It's brilliant."

"Isn't it? We should get our engineering department to work on the technical side as soon as possible. And I can start putting feelers out to our friends in the Funny Firm."

"The Funny Firm?"

Terry laughed.

"Old Met nickname for MI5. And with the game we've been playing with all the various law-enforcement agencies, I'm sure we've been noticed already."

"I do want to talk about intelligence."

"Good. It'll be a good move, believe me. Becoming an intelligence asset can secure certain, shall we say, accommodations. And working for the spooks, even on a completely unofficial and absolutely deniable manner, well, it puts you on another level entirely. It gives you a contact that's way beyond the security clearance of the police or any other of those other busybodies looking into your affairs. And we've got so much to offer them. Really high-end intelligence. Plus, help with black ops, dirty tricks, and what our Russian friends call *kompromat*. They need people like us for when the game gets dirty."

"Sounds good."

"Yes. I told you that by breaking Spinks's code you could become a man most mighty. This could make you an entirely new kind of operator."

Terry grasped Eddie's elbow and led him back over to the window, the other hand pointing with his cane at the city that stretched out eastwards below them, the river snaking voluptuously towards its vast estuary.

"See?" he declared as he blindly gestured at the sprawl below. "Intelligence, information, whatever you want to call it. Knowledge itself has become the biggest criminal enterprise of them all. All the dirty secrets of the world: think what they're worth. And soon you can start working on a political level."

"Political?"

"You know, offering your services to campaign strategists, things like that. The affairs of state, Eddie. A little influence there goes a long way, believe me. It can give you real protection."

Eddie sighed and shook his head slowly. He felt a distant pain building in his mind. Knowledge, he thought desperately. Yes, that's what he needed.

"I need something more simple from you, Terry," he said.

"I don't like the sound of that."

"The truth about something."

"Oh, Christ. You know what the divine Oscar said about truth, darling? That it's rarely pure and *never* simple. You shouldn't waste your time trying to find out the 'truth about something.' That's not what intelligence is about."

"No?"

"No. Trust me, it so rarely concerns itself with the actual truth about anything. It's about how you analyse data, trends, tendencies. It's about how you *use* facts. Manipulate them. How you can turn information into disinformation.

That's the big swindle to be played, Eddie. In the end, it's not intelligence that's important. It's counterintelligence."

"That all sounds very clever, Terry. But I just want to find something out."

"Don't."

"What?"

"Just don't. Remember when we first met, I told you that there are some things best not knowing about?"

"Yeah." Eddie frowned. "But I haven't even told you what it is yet."

"You don't have to. I just know it's going to cause you grief. I warned you before: wisdom is a terrible thing when it brings no profit. I really shouldn't have come."

Terry turned and began to walk out of the office.

"Wait!" Eddie shouted after him. "I need to know who killed Lee Royle!"

"There." Terry stopped and sighed. "Well, you've gone and said it now. Couldn't you have just kept quiet and been none the wiser? If I just go home now, couldn't we just forget about it?"

"You know something, don't you?"

"What if I do?"

"And you're not letting on."

"No."

Eddie went up to Terry and grabbed him by the suit lapels. "I need to know."

"Well, I'm not telling."

"Why not?"

"That's my business."

"Tell me, you dirty old queen!" He shook him roughly. "You miserable queer!"

Terry began to laugh. Eddie threw him to the floor.

"You're one to talk, Eddie Pierce," Terry drawled as he struggled for his cane.

"What do you mean?"

"I just wouldn't be so judgmental on sexual matters, if I were you."

"What?" Eddie put his foot against Terry's throat. "Don't play games with me. Just tell me what you know."

"You can rage all you like, Eddie. I won't tell you anything more."

"You had something to do with it, didn't you? I remember now; you knew all about it before anybody else. If you weren't just a blind old bastard, I'd say you did it yourself. But you must have had accomplices."

"Blind bastard, hmm, such choice insults, Eddie. But, you know, you're only seeing your own future."

"Tell me!" Eddie drew his foot back and kicked Terry in the ribs.

Terry groaned sharply and curled up in a spasm as Eddie stood above him seething. The old man retched up a mouthful of bile onto the carpet.

"It's all…" He panted, catching his breath. "It's all…just…a bit too close to home. Isn't it?"

"Craig," said Eddie suddenly, as if Terry had fed him a clue. "I knew it. It was Craig. He thought he could run things with Lee out of the way. You plotted together, didn't you? You're working for him; admit it."

"Oh, Eddie," Terry gasped, now on his hands and knees, clutching his cane.

"I'll get that bastard to talk. Don't you worry."

"Don't be ridiculous. I'm not working for Craig."

"I'll find out what happened," Eddie muttered darkly to himself. "And when I do–"

Terry was on his feet by now, brushing himself down, adjusting his dark glasses. He pulled the handkerchief from his top pocket and dabbed it against his lips.

"Eddie" – he shook his head slowly – "my dear boy. You've really lost it, haven't you?"

"Just go," Eddie said quietly, impatiently.

"This is a bloody tragedy; you know that, don't you? You could have it all. A whole kingdom in your grasp. And you're ready just to fucking blow it."

"Get out!" Eddie shouted.

Terry started to say something else, then thought better of it. Instead, he shrugged sadly, turned, and walked out of the office.

31

It was a simple plan, Jo decided. A straightforward way to distract Eddie from this unhealthy fixation in finding Lee's killer. It had been running through her head all day, slowly forming in her mind. The beauty of it was that she could use it for her own purposes, to solve a mystery of her own.

Gabriela came through to the kitchen to see her.

"Annie's asleep upstairs, if you want to check."

"No, it's all right."

Gabriela frowned. Jo usually made some fuss or other over the baby.

"It's OK," Jo reassured her.

She smiled at the nanny. Gabriela had witnessed how anxious Jo had been after the birth. How she'd first found it so hard to properly bond with her child, then become over-protective. Alert to any sign, no matter how insignificant, that something might be wrong. She had held on tight, while all the time been scared of getting too close. Now, Jo wanted Gabriela to know she was coming through it all. That she was getting better. She went to the fridge and got out an opened bottle of Chardonnay.

"I'm going to have a glass of wine, Gaby. Do you want one?"

Gabriela's eyes widened for an instant. Then she smiled.

"Yes," she said. "Why not?"

Jo poured them both a glass and they sat on stools by the central island.

"You're happy, Jo. Yes?"

"Yes. And look, Gaby, I'm going to need you to look after Annie more from now on."

"Really?"

"Yeah. I'm going back to work."

Jo knew that now was the time for her to get back in the game. Eddie had been under far too much stress over the past few months; it had made him obsessive and paranoid. She worried about him making the wrong decisions. And how power changed him. It seemed to make monsters out of men. Things would be so much better if they could get back to running things together.

She heard the front gate buzzer and the distant gravel drone of the driveway. She went to the window and saw Eddie's black Jaguar F-Pace speeding its way towards the house.

"I'd better get on," Gabriela said as she stood up and finished her wine.

Eddie padded tensely into the kitchen, a look of quiet fury on his face.

"You want a white wine, babe?" Jo asked him.

"Yeah," he breathed. "Fucking Terry Rice."

"What's the matter?" She poured him a glass.

"He knows something. But he's not telling."

"I don't understand."

"About Lee's killing."

"You asked him about that?"

"Yeah."

"What did you want to go and do that for?"

"He knows things, Jo. He knows everything. You said yourself."

"I was exaggerating a bit. Look, he's a genius at all that dark arts stuff, but that doesn't mean he can solve this thing."

"He's a fucking mine of information, that's for sure."

"Perhaps. But maybe you're not going to get what you want from him."

"I know that."

"So, I've got a better idea."

"Yeah." Eddie took a sip of wine. "So have I."

"Wait, just listen for a minute."

"OK. What?"

"Why don't we get a real expert on the subject?"

"What do you mean?"

"Hire a professional," Jo explained. "A private investigator."

"A private investigator?"

"Yeah. There's this guy I know. Dave Shephard. Lee used him from time to time. He's good. Ex-Old Bill. Really good detective skills. He could look at the whole thing afresh."

"I don't know about that."

"Well, let's face it, you're not going to find out who killed Lee through Terry Rice."

"No." Eddie slammed the glass on the work surface. "He's holding back on us. But I know someone else we could get it out of."

"What? Who?"

"Your fucking brother, that's who."

"What? Craig?"

"Yeah. I think him and Terry Rice were both involved. And now they're plotting against me."

"You're fucking joking."

"I'm absolutely serious."

Jo struggled to think. Eddie was starting to become delusional. She had to be careful about how she challenged him; contradictions could merely fuel his sense of persecution. She had to measure out the words that might make sense to him.

"Look," she tried to slow everything down. "Look, that's all the more reason to hire this detective guy, isn't it? Then we can be really sure of what happened. And what's going on."

He glared at her coldly and let out an ugly, mirthless laugh.

"Eddie?" she touched his arm.

His phone went and he brushed her hand away. He pulled the device out of his pocket and stared at its screen with a smile.

"There's another way of dealing with this," he told her as he accepted the call and clasped the mobile closely to the side of his face.

"Yeah?" he said, turning away from her. "You got him?… Right…OK…Yeah, take him to the lock-up in Dartford…I'll be there in half an hour."

He ended the call.

"Right." He stood up and started to walk out of the kitchen. "Got some business to attend to."

"Just hang on a minute!" she shouted after him, but he was soon out of the house.

As she heard him start the engine, Jo sighed heavily, for a moment relieved that he had gone and taken his dark mood with him. Then she realised what might be happening. She picked up her own car keys.

"Keep an eye on things here," she called to Gabriela as she headed for the front door. "I've got to go out for a bit."

32

Jamal watched as the bound and hooded figure was dragged across the concrete floor of the lock-up. He followed as the writhing body was hauled into a chair in the middle of the space, beneath the nervous buzz of a fluorescent strip light. He pulled off the cloth sack that covered its face.

"Wha–?" gasped Craig, blinking against the sudden brightness. "Wha...what the fuck are you doing?"

Eddie had ordered him taken. So Jamal had hunted him down with Tyrone and Jay, two heavyset brothers of his known association, well tutored in the profession of violence. They had grabbed him as he came out of his gym in Bexleyheath, bundled him into the boot of a car, and brought him to this industrial unit.

Craig's eyes flickered wildly between the brothers as they took either side of him and began to tie him down.

"Who the fuck are these guys?" he demanded.

"They work for me."

"But *you* work for *me*, Jamal. Remember?"

"Well, I'm taking my orders direct from Eddie at the moment."

Craig nodded slowly.

"Right," he said, chewing at his lower lip. "That's how it is, is it?"

"Yeah. That's how it is."

There came a clatter of someone knocking on the metal door. Jamal went to answer it as Tyrone and Jay loomed over Craig. He sneered at them.

"Go fuck yourselves," he muttered.

They smiled and backed away a little at the sound of footsteps on concrete. A shadow was cast in front of them as Eddie stepped into the light.

"You've got a fucking nerve, Craig," he said.

"What's this about, Eddie?"

"You know. Your plan to stab me in the back. I'd just like to know how you thought you'd get away with it? Did you somehow imagine that I wouldn't eventually work out what you were up to? Just what sort of a cunt do you take me for?"

Eddie nodded to Tyrone, who stepped forward.

"Look," Craig began, "I never–"

Tyrone punched the bound man hard in the stomach. Craig squealed as he doubled over in pain.

"Don't waste your breath if you're going to come up with some fairy story," Eddie insisted, and gestured to Jay, who now took his turn, landing a hard right cross on Craig's jaw.

"I need to know who killed Lee. You had something to do with it, didn't you?"

Craig spat blood and tried to catch his breath.

"The whole thing was some sort of set up, wasn't it?" Eddie went on. "Now I'm next on your list."

"No!"

"That's the plan, isn't it? You got rid of Lee. Now it's my turn."

"That's crazy."

"Is it?"

Craig frowned, his face screwed up in pain and incomprehension. He looked up at Eddie, whose expression seemed twisted in its own mad grimace. Craig closed his eyes and tried to think of a way of making sense to this man. He let out a sharp breath.

"Can I ask you something?" he pleaded softly.

"What?"

"Did you marry my sister?"

"Don't fuck around with me."

"Answer me. Did you marry my sister?"

"Yes. I did. What of it?"

"Well, I was happy with that, wasn't I? And happy with you taking over the firm? Of how you run things with Jo?"

"Well, we're equal partners, if that's what you mean. And we both thought we could trust you."

"Don't you see? You can! I've never wanted to be the boss. I'm not that guy, never have been. It was the same for all those years with Lee. I've never wanted all that grief that comes with being in charge. I get enough reward just being the right-hand man. And enough respect, too. Because I've earned it. I'm loyal, Eddie. I was loyal to Lee and I'm loyal to you. Ask anyone. Don't just act on your suspicions because you think I've been double-crossing you. Prove it, if you can. But take a bit of time, yeah? Then you'll find out the truth."

Eddie frowned and looked over at Jamal.

"He's got a point, bruv," said Jamal. "You don't want to be too fucking hasty."

"Oh, so I've just got to wait around while he does the dirty on me?" Eddie reached out with an open palm. "Give me your gun."

Jamal pulled out an automatic pistol from a shoulder holster and handed it to Eddie. He levelled the weapon at Craig's face.

"I want the truth. Did you kill Lee?"

"No."

"Then who did?"

"I don't know."

"You must have some idea. He had plenty of enemies."

"Yeah."

"Which one was it then?"

"I told you. I've no idea."

"OK." Eddie seethed out a breath. "Who did he fear the most?"

"Lee?" Craig made a bitter grin. "Oh, Lee didn't fear anyone."

"No?"

"Oh, no. He reckoned he was lucky, see? Thought he was charmed after getting a self-defence verdict on that copper. Didn't think anyone could get him except…"

Craig shrugged.

"What?" Eddie demanded.

"Just something he said one night. We'd been drinking, and I got round to asking if he was worried about Ipsworth coming after him, and he told me he wasn't scared of that slag. Then he said something weird. Said the only thing he was scared of was the killer inside."

"The what?"

"The killer inside. His "blood rival", he called them."

"Blood rival? What's that's supposed to mean?"

"Fuck knows. We'd been caning it all night, so his mind was all over the place."

There came a loud banging on the metal door of the unit.

"Are we expecting anybody else?" Eddie asked Jamal.

"No."

"Well, go and see who it is."

Jamal nodded to Tyrone, and they walked out to the front together.

"And you're going to tell me all about what you're up to," Eddie aimed the gun at Craig's face.

"I don't know what the fuck you're talking about."

"I want the truth, Craig."

"Oh, for fuck's sake!"

There was a commotion at the entrance of the lock-up, but the two men were so absorbed in argument they paid it no heed.

"Admit it!" Eddie insisted. "Admit that you're trying to have me over!"

"What, so you can kill me?"

"Yes." He pressed the barrel against Craig's forehead.

"Wait!" Jo shouted as she strode up towards the huddle of men that turned to face her. "Just what the fuck is going on?"

Craig laughed as Eddie pulled the pistol away and turned to face Jo.

"He wants to kill me, sis."

"What the fuck?" She glared at the gun in Eddie's hand, now loosely pointed at her. "Give me that."

He handed the weapon to her, and as she took it with her left hand, she slapped him hard across the face with her right.

"What the hell do you think you're doing?"

"He's up to something." Eddie rubbed his cheek.

"On my life, Jo. I've never done nothing against either of you. I swear."

"Eddie?"

"I don't trust him."

"Why not?"

"There's something up," he insisted. "I just know it."

"How?"

"I don't know. It's a gut feeling."

Jo came closer.

"And that makes you act like this?" she whispered hoarsely at him. "Like a fucking lunatic? You've got to get your act together, and quickly. This is madness."

"But what if he did have something to do with Lee's murder?" he murmured grimly.

"All the more reason," she said softly to him. "To do what I said before."

Eddie thought for a moment, then sighed.

"OK," he told them all. "Let him go."

"I mean it," Jo said as Craig was being untied. "Let's have this thing properly looked into. Before you lose it completely and kill somebody. What's the matter with you?"

Craig stood up and flexed his wrists, rubbing at where the rope had chafed, wiping his mouth with the back of his hand. He looked over at his accuser who glared angrily back at him.

"Go on, get out," Eddie told him. "Just think yourself lucky your sister stood up for you."

Craig shook his head slowly.

"This is out of order, Eddie. You know that."

"Just fuck off!"

Craig began to walk out. At the doorway, he turned back to look at them all.

"Just remember, I'm still running the roads and the county lines. I've got a lot of friends in Kent that know me for what I am. I've got a lot of respect from them. And I deserve a lot more from you."

The metal door slammed behind him. Eddie stood brooding in the shadows. Jo went up to Jamal and handed him the automatic pistol.

"How on earth did all of this kick off?" she asked him.

"He just went into one over Craig. Ordered me to bring him here."

"Right."

She looked over at Eddie. He had one hand clasped against his face.

"Keep all of this quiet," she told Jamal. "And I'll try and patch things up with Craig. We don't want everybody thinking my husband's losing it."

The fury she felt at Eddie's behaviour began to ebb a little as she noted how distraught he seemed. She went over and put an arm around his shoulder.

"Come on, babe," she murmured in his ear. "Let's go home."

33

Jo came downstairs to find Eddie sitting in the kitchen, nursing a large brandy.

"How's Annie?" he asked her.

"Still asleep. She slept through all of it. What's this?"

She had spotted the bottle of pills by the glass in front of Eddie. She picked it up and read the label.

"Almotryptan? What the hell is this, Eddie?"

"For my headaches. I went to a doctor."

"A doctor?"

"A neurologist. A specialist in Harley Street."

"And you didn't think of telling me?"

"Didn't want to worry you. Thought I might have a brain tumour or something. But they couldn't find anything."

"Christ, Eddie. What's happening? And this thing with Craig. You know it's out of order."

"Is it?"

"Of course it is. This is what's driving you crazy. All these thoughts about Lee's murder."

"Craig said something strange."

"What?

"He said Lee *was* scared of somebody. Something about a blood rival."

"Oh." Jo started a little.

"What do you think he meant by that?"

"I've no idea," she lied, a little too quickly.

"Jo?" he squinted at her and took a sip of brandy.

"I don't know, Eddie. Lee was full of secrets. Like that thing with Chris Ipsworth. That bastard was an enigma. I wish we could just forget him and get on with our own lives."

But the blood rival was one mystery that she did know about. The killer inside he had ranted about while on remand. All the threats he had made with that strange terror in his eyes. Forcing her to do that terrible thing.

"What is it, Jo?"

Eddie gazed over at her, his eyes bleary with drugs and alcohol. She would tell him soon, she decided. Once she had pieced everything together for herself. She wanted to know the whole story first.

"Nothing," she told him. "Just a bit rattled by what happened today. We both need to get some rest. You're all wired up."

"Yeah."

"And I'm pretty sure your doctor didn't say you could drink on that medication."

"No." Eddie picked up the glass, glared at it, then drained it in one.

Jo sighed.

"What else did the doctor say?"

Eddie laughed softly.

"Not much. Said I should go and see a shrink. You know, psychotherapy. It could be all some hidden trauma in the past, he reckons. Something from an unhappy childhood, I suppose."

"Maybe."

"Thing is Jo, I had a good upbringing."

"Yeah."

"But see how I turned out." He grinned.

"Eddie."

"My parents did all they could to make me happy. But for some reason, I resented them for it. I always thought there was something wrong. With me."

"What do you mean?"

"I don't know. All I know is, it wasn't their fault."

"Who?"

"My parents. I've never told you much about them, have I?"

"I know they threw you out when you got into trouble."

"No. It wasn't like that."

"No?"

"No."

"But you lost contact with them after youth detention."

"That was my choice. It was my decision to get out of their lives, not theirs. I knew I couldn't go home. I was just so full of this rage. And I still don't know why. It was as if something terrible might happen if I went back there."

"Really?"

"Yeah. And for such a long time I didn't feel I belonged anywhere. Until I met you, of course."

"Right." She smiled.

"It's true. There *was* something wrong with me back then. And I was completely off the rails. A mid-range drug dealer, getting high on his own supply. The things I got up to. Sometimes I was so out of it, I'd have these blackouts, you know? Where I couldn't quite remember what had happened."

"God."

"Yeah. I was lost, Jo. Before you, I was fucking lost."

"Oh, babe."

"But now, you're my family. You and Annie."

"And Craig."

"Yeah, well…"

"Like it or not, Eddie. You're going to have to make peace with my brother. As you said, we're family, right? So we've got to stick together. There are plenty of rival firms out there ready to move in if they know we're falling out with each other."

"And that's why we need to sort out what happened with Lee. It's the uncertainty of it, you know? That's the worst of it. And it's an uncertainty that people could take advantage of. It's like we can't protect our own."

"OK, so let's get professional help. This private investigator."

"I'm not sure if I want an outsider dealing with our business."

"Well, he might be something of an insider, too."

"What do you mean?"

"He's ex-police. He'll have ways of finding out some of the internal details of the investigation. Stuff that Kent CID have been keeping to themselves."

"You sure about that?"

"Oh, yes. That was Dave Shepherd's speciality back in the day. That's what Lee used him for. He's got some good contacts in the Job. If anyone can dig up what's known about the murder, he can."

"Well, give him a call."

"He might even be able to trace this eyewitness."

"What?"

"You know, that Asian detective said something about it. That there was supposed to be this eyewitness. At Junction 1A."

"Eyewitness," Eddie repeated flatly, staring out at nothing for a moment, as if in a trance. "Junction 1A."

"Eddie?" she shook him gently.

His glazed eyes suddenly blinked, then focussed on her.

"What?"

"Christ, Eddie. You're really out of it. Come on." She stood up. "Let's go to bed."

"Right," he muttered, as she led him to the staircase.

"You've got to get it together, babe," she whispered, as they staggered up together.

And she knew that they would have to make this work. Soon, he would know the harsh truth about her past. She needed him to be mentally stable to cope with that.

That night, Jo curled up around him on the bed, in the half-sleep that awaits an infant's call on the baby alarm. She sought refuge in that part-oblivion, hoping for simple comfort, with no worries of the future. To hide from the starry sky and all of its fateful constellations. But a restless world turned, marking another night. Another day closer to destiny.

34

Jo met him at the front door. *Same old Dave Shepherd*, she thought as he swaggered through in his Paul Smith suit and open-necked shirt. Still playing the flash bastard. And she knew just how to use that to get him on her side.

"Hello, handsome," she greeted him with a smile.

His eyes lit up as he took both of her hands in his.

"Well, Jo," he told her. "You're looking great. As ever."

"Not looking so bad yourself, Dave," she assured him.

The fact was that he'd gone to seed. His face had become jowly, and he'd thickened out all over. But she knew that this man fancied himself so much he wouldn't think to question her flattering comment for a moment. He had that confidence of vanity that made him unselfconscious.

And he'd never realised that she flirted with him out of boredom. She found his brash demeanour a bit ridiculous – funny, even. Over the years, it had entertained her to play this silly game with him. Now she knew she could use it to her advantage.

"How's business?" she asked.

"Well, there's plenty of it. Corporate security, surveillance, bailiff work, repossessions. Good money, but not very exciting. Be glad to be doing a bit of proper detective work."

"Well, you're the man for the job, Dave."

JAKE ARNOTT   201

"I certainly am, Jo." He grinned, with a twinkle in his eye. "I certainly am."

Jo forced a stupid little giggle as Eddie descended the stairs into the hallway.

"All right?" came his harsh greeting.

They broke hands and turned to face him. Jo noted how troubled Eddie looked. He'd still not been sleeping well and had been in a dark mood for much of the day. The headaches persisted. His face was an ugly scowl.

"This is my husband," she told Dave as Eddie approached.

"Lucky man," said Dave breezily.

"What?" Eddie snarled, as if affronted by the suggestion.

"Well, you've got a beautiful wife."

"Yeah. Let's get down to business, shall we?"

Dave stole another glance at Jo, raising his eyebrow. She flashed a quick grin but kept her eye on Eddie. She realised then that she would have to be careful how she worked this.

As he led them into the front room, Jo thought about how she'd messed about with Dave Shepherd in the past. Lee hadn't seemed to mind; he'd almost appeared to encourage it. But back then, she had been the trophy wife, something to be shown off in male company. It was as if Lee got some vicarious thrill from this, that her desirability enhanced his own sense of power.

She caught Eddie's stare, and it struck her how different her second husband was. He had little interest in how she might be objectified by some curious gaze. His desire for her was simple: fierce, direct, and jealously protective.

"So," he said brusquely as they sat down, "Jo's told you about the job."

"Yes," Dave replied, "and I've had a quick look at the case. Let me tell you what I've got so far."

Shepherd went through some of the details of the investigation he thought hadn't been properly followed up. Although the killing had happened at a CCTV blind spot, there hadn't been a very thorough examination of other video evidence from that junction. There should have been a check on all vehicles that might have been driving to or from the area of the incident over a fixed timescale. This was mind-numbingly laborious work that a lazy officer might easily have skipped over. And the forensic check had been cursory as well. The stabbing of Lee had been identified as a brief attack, and it was not expected that it would leave many discernible traces.

"The thing is," Dave went on, "the Leyton Cross shootings came along so quickly, and that really swallowed up resources for the murder team."

Jo looked over at Eddie. His eyes flared a moment at the mention of the killings, but he remained stony faced.

"So they were cutting corners on Lee's case?" he demanded.

"That's one way of looking at it," Dave reasoned. "But all police work does have to be budgeted for."

"As I told my case worker," Jo added. "The police were never going to waste too much time and effort finding Lee's murderer."

"Who was that?" Dave asked. "The case worker, I mean."

"I don't know. Asian woman. A DC, I think."

"Detective Constable Meera Hussain," Eddie announced.

Jo looked over at him with a puzzled frown.

"She gave me a card," he explained.

"Well, I can look out for her," Dave went on. "But look,

once the investigation team decided it was probably an unidentified assailant not known to Lee Royle, well, it means we don't really have any clear suspect to look at, or even a profile."

"What if I was to give you one?" asked Eddie.

"Who?"

"Craig Cadmoor."

"Eddie," Jo protested.

"Even if it's just to rule him out," he insisted. "What would you do?"

"I'd start with his statement. Look for any discrepancies. In fact, I'd do that with all the statements. And see if anything was left out."

"I doubt if they missed much in all the interviews," said Eddie.

"You'd be surprised," Dave countered. "You see, once they'd fixed on the road rage angle, it gives them a very linear course of investigation. They might not have followed up anything tangential."

"So, you're just going to go through all the statements, looking for discrepancies?"

"You never know what might turn up."

"Hmm." Eddie stood up. "I was hoping for something a little more proactive, not just going through the paperwork and seeing if anything has been left out. That looks like just going through the motions to me."

For a moment, Jo feared that Eddie would change his mind about hiring Dave. Then her whole plan would be scuppered. She smiled at the detective, willing him to come up with something.

"There is the eyewitness, of course," he said, as if reading her mind.

"Yeah." Eddie nodded thoughtfully. "The eyewitness. But the police never managed to trace them."

"There might still be a way. And it's worth checking on the information that they gave, anyway. They saw a red sports car, apparently."

"A red sports car?"

"Yeah," Dave chuckled. "Maybe the murderer was going through a mid-life crisis."

Jo laughed along at this, but Eddie frowned, as if narrowing his gaze on something.

"A red sports car," he repeated.

"If we can find a match with any of the CCTV footage and get a number plate reading."

"Or, if you could track down the eyewitness," Eddie suggested.

Dave nodded.

"I think there's a lot of lines of inquiry that I can follow," he told them.

So it was agreed that he would take the job. Jo was relieved, though Eddie's mood didn't brighten. His face was set in a grim mask, growing quieter as the conversation continued, nodding morosely as Shepherd began to wind things down. Dave explained the basic logistics of how he would work with them, that he knew the senior investigating officer. He could try to access all the relevant police files, though that might be quite costly in payoffs. Eventually, the private investigator stood up.

"Right, then," he said. "I'll be off."

"Yeah," Eddie responded softly, scarcely looking up.

"I'll see you out, Dave," said Jo.

They walked to his car together. This was the time to make her pitch, she decided.

"Well, your new bloke," Dave said quietly. "Bit intense, isn't he?"

"He's under a lot of pressure."

"I guess."

"It's good to see you, Dave. Glad that you'll be working for us."

"Me too. Though, to be honest," he sighed wistfully, "I wish I was just working for you, Jo."

She stopped in her tracks, glancing back at the house for a moment, then turning to him. *Now,* she thought, as she took hold of his arm.

"What if you were?"

"What?"

"Working just for me. On another job."

"Another job?"

"Something very simple. But you've got to keep it secret. Completely on the down low."

"What is it?"

"I want you to find someone for me."

"A missing person?"

"Not exactly."

"What, then?"

"Look, I can't talk about this here. Get started on this thing and I'll come to your office in the week. But Dave, listen…" She pulled at his arm a little, to bring him closer to her. "No one's to know about this."

"Right." He nodded, suddenly a little flustered. "Not even Eddie?"

"Especially not Eddie."

She brought her face close to his, caught the scent of sweat and aftershave.

"Something just between us," she whispered in his ear. "OK?"

Then she let go of his arm and he got into his car. And she watched him drive away.

Jo turned back to the house with a determined smile. Now she could get things started. Face her past, she thought, her gaze fixed on the gravel path. And she didn't look up all the way back to the house. She didn't see that Eddie had spied the whole of this intimate scene from an upstairs window.

35

It was when Meera Hussain noticed for the second time that someone had been tampering with the records of the Lee Royle case that she knew she had to act. She had long suspected that the investigation had been compromised, right from the start with that farcical business with Ray Spinks. Meera remained convinced that it was him that had leaked early details of the murder to the press. The Commander's own mysterious demise had hardly helped matters. Scotland Yard had managed to keep a lid on official speculation about this murky affair, but the rumours continued about a criminal relationship between Royle and Spinks.

And Eddie Pierce's remark that the inquiry into Royle's murder had been "not good enough" had stirred it all up in her mind once more. Pierce was one of the few people who seemed to care about finding Royle's killer. His widow, Jo, certainly hadn't expressed much grief over his murder. Indeed, there was certain indifference shown to this investigation, on both sides of the law. It seemed a lot of people wanted this matter not to be too closely looked at.

But somebody had certainly been interfering with the case records. The files had been boxed up and left in one corner of the incident room, ready to go into storage. First, she saw that one of the cardboard archive crates had been removed from the stack and left on its own, at an angle. Then, later in the week, she noted that a lid had been rather clumsily replaced and not properly secured.

So she decided to go and see her boss about it. She heard laughter coming from Detective Chief Inspector Creighton's office as she knocked on the door. Then a booming voiced entreating her to enter. Creighton sat at his desk in his shirtsleeves. A burly besuited man sat opposite and stood up as she came in.

"Sorry to interrupt, sir," she said.

"No problem." Creighton nodded to his guest. "Dave, this is Detective Constable Meera Hussain. Dave Shepherd. Used to be in the Job."

"Right," said Dave as he shook her hand, nodding slowly as if he recognised her from somewhere.

"Meera is one of the new intakes. We're all very politically correct now."

"Yeah." Dave let out a little laugh, as if this was some sort of a joke.

"And Dave runs a private investigation firm in Bromley," Creighton went on. "Used to be a bloody good thief-taker. We worked Regional Crime Squad together."

"Those were the days," Dave added.

"So, what can I do you for, Meera?"

"The Lee Royle files."

"Oh, right," Creighton said breezily, as if being reminded of something.

"Look, sir, I could come back later," she suggested.

Dave Shepherd grinned, taking the hint.

"I'd better be getting on, George," he said, and made for the door.

"Give me a call about that lunch," Creighton called after him. "Soon."

As the Detective Chief Inspector turned to her, she nearly laughed at his attempt at calm authority. There was an almost childlike look of guilt in his eyes.

"Look," he insisted, with involuntary petulance. "I was going to tell everyone on the team. Just been having a last look at the case. You know, a final once over before we put it to bed."

He patted a small pile of documents on his blotter. Meera could just make out that the top one was Craig Cadmoor's statement. As she looked up, she found herself glaring at her boss. As he caught her stare, Creighton's face hardened.

"Right, Hussain," he announced brusquely. "Why don't you bring all of it up to my office and Administration can come and collect it from here?"

"Yes, sir."

She stood stock still at his desk.

"Was there anything else?" he huffed at her with studied impatience.

Meera thought for a moment.

"No, sir."

But as she went through the menial errand of fetching and carrying all the files that related to the investigation, her mind recorded everything that looked wrong about the way the case had been conducted. She suspected a serious breach of operational security and intelligence handling. Standard operating procedure on information security certainly hadn't been followed. Confidentiality, integrity, and, indeed, availability might not have been preserved and protected. All these elements combined to indicate that dread reality that haunted every conscientious police officer: corruption.

Of course, the first thing you were advised to do upon suspecting something like this was to raise the matter discreetly with a superior officer. As she placed the last box on his office floor, she looked up at Detective Chief Inspector Creighton. Glaring down at her imperiously, as if goading her to say something.

Hussain knew that he had all but total control of her career path. He could transfer her almost anywhere. He could send her back to uniform.

"Thank you, Hussain," he said curtly. "That'll be all."

On her way back to her desk, she went through her other options. She could file a report to Kent Police's Professional Standards Department. It might be then dealt with by the Operational Security Officer who could then pass it on to the force's own Anti-Corruption Unit. Alternatively, she could take it to the local authority level, through the office of the Police and Crime Commissioner, or even nationally with the Independent Office of Police Conduct. All of these austere bodies were there ready to deal with this gut feeling she had that something had gone seriously wrong with a major investigation that she had been part of.

But the dilemma she now faced was that following any of these courses of action could so easily mess things up badly for her. She was liable to be viewed with disdain by her superiors and distrust by her colleagues. Forever marked as a whistleblower, a troublemaker, a grass. She just didn't feel she could take such a risk so early in her career in CID. She wanted to get on.

Besides, Creighton was clearly implicated, and it would be her word against a Detective Chief Inspector. She had already shown her hand, and he would have already begun to cover his tracks. And the officious manner with which he had her move the boxes was a simple demonstration of his power over her. He was keeping an eye on her, reminding her who was boss, that he could decide what her job was. That he could treat her like a filing clerk rather than a detective.

But she *was* a detective, Meera told herself. For now, at least. And nothing could stop her thinking like one.

So she thought about the case once more.

The one lead they had was the supposed eyewitness who had claimed to have seen a red sports car at the scene of the crime. But this was an uncorroborated testimony from an anonymous source, and one had to cautious with tip-offs like these. It could be the figment of somebody's imagination or even something more malignant. Withholding evidence is an obvious strategy in corrupting an investigation, but a more subtle method was to come up with false or misleading information to misdirect anyone looking at the case.

And this unidentified vehicle conveniently fit the official line that this was a random road-rage killing. But there were so many other threads, a bewildering labyrinth of tangential connections. The most common linking factor, of course, was Lee Royle's widow.

Meera recalled Jo's reaction to the news of Royle's death, that burst of embarrassed laughter. And she had been present at the Brian Colby murder scene in the hours after the man's death. Ray Spinks had called her a "clever bitch" and suggested putting her under covert surveillance.

Jo had the most to gain from Lee's demise, after all. Somehow, this woman was the key to something that would unlock everything, Meera decided, with no clear idea how she might prove this.

She wished now that they had put her under surveillance, though it wouldn't have been easy. Jo had always been wary and suspicious of the police, and contemptuous of their offers of protection after the Colby killing. Besides, running a surveillance operation used up a lot of resources and manpower.

And now Meera was on her own. There were few fellow officers she felt she could confide in. She might have gone to Cheryl Symons at Family Liaison, but she had just gone on leave. And she knew the rest of the team tended to see her as the token Asian woman who just tried a little bit too hard at everything. She felt compelled to do something, though, and it quickly came to her. It was her turn to dispense with standard operating procedure, she thought with a smile. Forget about officialdom and just get to the heart of the matter.

36

"Christ, Jo," Dave Shepherd whispered harshly when she had finished her story. "I had no idea about any of this."

"Nobody did. Except me and Lee. And I want to keep it that way."

"Of course," he said.

She had sat in his office and told him all the grim details from long ago.

"I mean..." There was a slight sob in her voice. "You can imagine how guilty I feel about it all."

"But it was Lee's idea. I mean, that's what you said."

"Yeah, but I went along with it, didn't I?" Jo sniffed.

It was then that she realised that she had been crying. She swiped at her eyes with the back of each hand. It was relief, more than anything else. That she could finally tell somebody what she had done.

Because she had felt sick with guilt and paranoia when she visited Dave Shepherd. She had told Eddie that she was going to Bromley to see a friend. Parked her distinctive pearl blue Mitsubishi Shogun a couple of blocks away, just to be sure.

"I still don't quite get Lee's motive in all this," Shepherd said.

"He was scared."

"Scared?"

"Yeah," she smiled. "A big tough man scared of something like that."

"That's fucked up."

"Isn't it?"

It had actually been easier than she thought to tell the private investigator what had happened. She didn't care about him that much, so she didn't worry about his reactions. And here, at last, was somebody that might be able to do something about it. She just wondered how much she could really trust him.

"The blood rival," she muttered.

"What?"

"That's what he really feared. The killer inside, he called it."

"Jesus. So all of this was when he was on trial for killing that undercover cop?"

"Yeah, and he was doing everything he could to get off. But this thing…" she shuddered.

"What?"

"A life for a life."

"You mean?"

"Yeah. He thought he was going to get life."

"And then he gets off with the self-defence plea."

"It was like some terrible bargain, Dave. Life? That's the fucking joke. I was the one that got life. Life with that cruel bastard. Life with the guilt of what I had done."

"And you kept quiet about it all this time."

"Yeah."

"Until Lee got killed."

"Well, that changed everything, didn't it?"

"It did, Jo," he sighed. "It did."

Dave Shepherd looked down with a thoughtful squint. His mind working through something.

"Jo." He looked up, peering at her across the desk. "I've got to ask you, what does this business have to do with Lee's murder?"

"Nothing. Why?"

"Well, you have asked me to investigate the killing. See what the police investigation missed."

"Yeah, but," she reasoned hurriedly, "that's for Eddie. I don't care who killed Lee. Eddie's the one that's worried about it."

"And why is he so worried?"

"I don't know. Maybe it's this thing about an unsolved murder. It's made him paranoid."

"That's understandable."

"But he's become suspicious of everyone."

"Even you?" he demanded.

She frowned. She hadn't thought of that.

"I don't know." Her voice was all at once full of doubt.

"Have you told him you don't care who murdered your last husband?"

"Yeah. I have, Dave. I don't care." Jo's tone was suddenly vehement. "In fact, I've told Eddie I'm glad Lee got done."

"I'd be careful who else you say that to."

"What?"

"Well." He pouted. "With what you've just told me…"

And as he leant back in his chair and folded his arms, Jo realised that she might have underestimated Dave Shepherd. He was a detective, after all. Always ready to think laterally.

"Yeah." She smiled, following his line of thought. "It does kind of give me a motive, doesn't it?"

"All I'm saying is that it's worth bearing that in mind, Jo. If anyone else finds out about what you're asking me to look into."

"Well, you've got to keep it secret."

"I'll do what I can."

"You've got to."

Jo stared at Dave Shepherd. She really did need to know how far she could trust him.

"I mean, you're right about motive," she went on, suddenly fearless. "I did want Lee dead. But I didn't kill him."

"No?"

"No." She smiled archly. "But what if I did? What would you do then?"

"What do you mean?"

All at once he looked nervous. She glared at him provocatively.

"I don't know." Jo shrugged. "Say you found something incriminating."

"About you?"

"Yeah."

"Well," he huffed. "That depends on what it was."

He tried to sound nonchalant, but she could tell he was flustered.

"You'd look after me, wouldn't you, Dave?" she spoke softly now, holding his gaze all the time.

"Yeah. Well." He nodded. "I'd do whatever I could."

"That's good." She beamed.

And Jo knew then that she had him where she wanted him. That she could trust him with her secret, and he would do what he was told.

"So," she went on. "I want you to go easy on how you look at Lee's murder inquiry. Go through the motions.

Keep Eddie happy, but don't worry too much about finding anything new."

"OK."

"And if you do, let me know about it first."

"Right."

"But it's this other thing I want you to concentrate on. I want this to take priority."

"That's fine. It shouldn't take too long, after all."

"Good. Because I want you to deal with it personally. I know you've got other staff but…"

"Don't worry. I won't let anyone else near it."

"I appreciate that, Dave," she breathed the words to him as she stood up to leave.

And as he walked her to the door, she let him kiss her gently on the cheek.

Outside, Jo felt light-headed, buzzing a little at how she had played Dave Shepherd. She smiled to herself at how easy he was to manipulate. It was a serious game she was playing, but she got a little high with it.

So she forgot herself for a moment and only made a cursory scan of the street as she walked out onto the pavement. She had been so careful coming here, checking all the time that no one had followed her car. But she hadn't noticed that Jamal had tailed her on foot. And that he had spotted her leaving Dave Shepherd's offices from the window seat of the café opposite.

37

Eddie headed northbound on the M25. Driving that familiar highway again. Back in orbit once more. It felt good to be on the road. Standing still just gave him vertigo. That fear of looking down on his own life.

And his ascent to power had been so swift. He had reached the top in a state of sickening imbalance. There was an awful uncertainty of what he would see if he gazed below. He imagined a terrible void down there, waiting to swallow him up. Yet he felt drawn to the edge, ready to jump. So a strange calm possessed him as moved so fast. Driving, his body relaxed, even while his head spun.

He was on his way to a meeting at Bluewater Shopping Centre. Jamal had called with some information on Jo, but Eddie hadn't wanted to talk long on the phone. Anybody could be listening in, even with an encrypted system. He realised with dread that Terry Rice could have hacked into his mobile.

And he had so many other enemies out there. Word had spread of his fallout with Craig, and there were rumours of a new syndicate ready to move in on his territory. He felt encircled by threat and betrayal, while his mind strafed with waves of pain. The drugs that his neurologist had prescribed weren't working anymore. They weren't strong enough to quell his thoughts of murder.

As he approached Junction 2 and the turn off for Bluewater, Eddie nearly stayed on the motorway. Something urged him to drive on to Junction 1A, to have a look at the crime scene once more. But he had to see Jamal first, so he took the exit on to the A2 that took him to the shopping centre.

Eddie parked up and walked to their arranged meeting point. He nodded to Jamal casually and they wandered together through a vast steel and glass atrium.

"We really do need to sort things out with Craig," Jamal told him as they mounted an escalator.

"Yeah," Eddie sighed. "But what have you got to tell me about Jo?"

"Well." He shrugged. "She was at Dave Shepherd's offices between three and three-thirty yesterday afternoon."

"Right. You saw her coming out?"

"Yeah."

"What did she look like?"

"Look like? How do you mean, bruv?"

They reached the upper plaza and stepped out onto a walkway of polished stone. A parade of retail chains. Fast food. Fast fashion.

"Her expression. What was her expression like?" Eddie demanded.

"I don't know."

"Have a go."

"Happy." Jamal nodded thoughtfully. "Yeah, she had a smile on her face."

"Right."

Eddie led them both over to the railings. He looked down at the tiered galleries below.

"First off, I want you to get someone to break into Dave Shepherd's premises," he said. "Bug the place up. Get his door codes, his alarm system."

"Might not be that easy, you know? He's a private investigator, after all. Bound to have good security."

"Just get it done, OK? You must know someone who can do this."

"Hmm." He nodded. "I do."

"And keep an eye on her."

"Jo?"

"Yeah. Round-the-clock surveillance. I want to know her every move."

"OK."

Eddie looked up at the widely arched roof of the shopping mall. The sun refracted harshly through its tinted glass. He turned back to Jamal.

"So," he said, "have you got that other thing?"

Jamal sighed and took out a bottle of pills and handed it over. Eddie read the label. OXYCONTIN 15mg.

"You want to be careful with those," Jamal told him. "They're really powerful."

"That's what I need. Something that can deal with these fucking headaches."

"But listen, go easy. They're not supposed to be addictive, but they are. You know what they call them in the States? Hillybilly heroin."

"Yeah, well."

"I'm worried about you, bruv."

"What, you think I'm losing it or something?"

"No, but…"

"Just get on with your job, Jamal. I'm all right."

In the car park, Eddie felt his phone buzz in his pocket. He pulled it out and looked at the screen. No name, just a number he couldn't quite recognise. A landline that triggered some distant memory. He let it go to voicemail. As he pocketed the mobile, his hand felt the pill bottle. He grabbed it, rattled out a couple of tablets and gulped them down.

In the car, he put his mobile on speakerphone and played the message back.

"Eddie," came a plaintive voice from the past. It registered in his guts.

Christ, he thought. This is all I fucking need right now.

"It's your mother," came that doleful intonation he knew so well. "There's been some bad news. Please call me."

Then just her breath. Her mournful breath.

"I miss you," she let out a short *huh* sound. "I love you."

And then she ended the call.

He took a circuitous route back. Following B roads and suburban streets that lined the river. The bridge loomed beyond at the Dartford Crossing. He passed a retail park, then was in open country.

For a moment, he seemed lost in the tranquil pastures of Kent. It was a bright summer's day, a rural idyll. But as he approached Junction 1A, his thoughts became ominous once more. *Yes*, he brooded, *driving is destiny*. He put his foot down. Speed, that's what he needed. He felt it accelerating him towards some grim purpose.

Jo. She was betraying him too. Terry Rice, Craig, and now her. They were all against him. And it cut so deep into him that she might turn against him like this. He could hardly believe it. Then a terrible logic took hold of him. That this had been her intention all along.

She had wanted Lee dead, after all. More than anyone. *A bit too close to home*, that's what Terry Rice had said when he'd pressed him on the identity of the murderer. He meant her. She was this blood rival Craig had spoken of. Maybe she had got somebody to kill Lee and make it look like road rage. She would have known his movements that day. Only Jo could have planned something as meticulously as that.

So perhaps the whole thing had been a set up right from the start. She had always planned for him to take the fall for her. Maybe the others were in on it too. It was Craig that ordered him to mind Jo in the first place. Right after that, Terry Rice had conveniently got in touch. And the murder of the lawyer Brian Colby, perhaps his first instincts were right about that, too. That she had intended him to be found with the murder weapon and at the scene.

And just as he had tried to find out about Lee's murder, she had been the one that tried to stop him. Now she was secretly meeting this ex-cozzer, with friends on the investigation team. Was she using Dave Shepherd to fit him up for the killing?

Eddie tried to banish such ugly thoughts from his mind. That she might have used him like this, and the depths she had gone to. He didn't want to believe it. But an evil reasoning compelled him onwards. He felt he was getting closer to an awful truth.

He began to slow down as he approached the traffic intersection: Junction 1A, a crossroads of destiny. This was where it all happened. This was where it all might be revealed.

It was then that the drugs kicked in. As he followed the exit that Lee must have taken that morning, Eddie felt the rush of powerful opioids within. A surge of endorphins unlocked from the synapses of his brain. It came like an epiphany.

And when he turned down that fateful slip road, he had an out-of-body experience. His consciousness floating freely, finding itself on the embankment above. Looking down, he saw it all so clearly. The vehicles pulled up against each other. The two men on the tarmac, in a dance of death.

It was like a video that could be run forwards or backwards. Or a computer game. Yes. Like Gran Turismo he had on his PlayStation, where you could select a car to race and its colour. Here was a Land Rover Discovery. Dark blue. And the little sports car? He flicked through his mind as if viewing options on a screen. Yes, he decided. It was a Mazda MX-5. Bright red.

Just then, a car behind him blared its horn. He was going too slowly. So he pulled away and began to make his way back to West Kingsdown. His mind coming back to its corporeal self. His thoughts coalescing.

He let out a long breath and nearly laughed out loud. It all seemed so absurd. Maybe *he* had been the eyewitness. The anonymous bystander that had made that call to the police. But how could that be? He didn't even have a car that morning. How could he have got to Junction 1A?

But perhaps he was another kind of eyewitness. One that looked beyond. Drug psychosis had now given him a feeling of omniscience, and suddenly he thought himself gifted with a second sight. Like Terry Rice, he could see it all. And as he drove home, he began to brood on how he might use this new power to his advantage.

It was still a bright afternoon when he arrived back at Sevengates. Jo was in the garden with Annie. His wife in a summer dress, their baby in a Moses basket, sitting together in the orchard. A pastoral scene he could not feel part of. He wanted to get away from the light and find shadow.

"Hi," he said and forced a smile.

She frowned and he realised how ghastly his face must look. Twisted, like his mind that had been turning over and over. He was mentally exhausted.

"Eddie," she entreated softly, "are you OK?"

A look of concern on her face. Or was it just suspicion?

"I'm wiped out," he told her. "I need a rest."

"All right." She stood up and went to hold him.

But he froze to her touch.

"What's the matter?"

"Nothing. Just need some sleep."

The pity of it all was that he still loved her, he thought, as he wandered into the house. He still wanted her with a burning desire. But that's what had trapped him. Some primitive lust that had drawn them together from the start. Some savage passion with no pity. He couldn't trust her. She might be as ruthless with him as she had been with Lee.

He went to the bedroom and undressed. He lay on the bed, closing his eyes and willing his brain to follow the calm darkness of a dream. The voice of his mother came once more. *I miss you,* she had said. *I love you.* But what did she want now? *There's been some bad news,* she had said. What could that mean?

He thought about the eyewitness once more. In his delirium, this anonymous source had become something transcendental. An all-seeing eye to guide him. He wondered what to do with the knowledge it seemed to give him.

He rolled over on the bed to reach for his jacket on the floor. He found his wallet and pulled out the crumpled card with a Kent Police crest on it. DETECTIVE CONSTABLE MEERA HUSSAIN it read, with a phone number and email address.

38

She flashed her warrant card when the receptionist asked if she had an appointment and stormed in to find him at his desk. He looked up and smiled.

"And what can I do for you, Detective Constable Hussain?" Dave Shepherd's voice was pitched somewhere between indignation and bemused charm.

"I just want to know what the fuck is going on."

He laughed.

"What do you mean?"

"You know."

"Look." He shrugged. "I'm just helping your guvnor out a bit, in a consultative capacity. You understand? You heard what George said: one last look before we cold case it."

"This is completely out of order."

"Yeah," he drawled lazily. "I suppose it is. So what are you doing here? Shouldn't you be reporting all of this to professional standards?"

"Well, I, um…" Meera tried to put together some sort of excuse for her action, or lack of it, and then gave up.

Her face said it all. And his conceited grin told her that he knew it.

"Nobody wants to be a whistleblower," he told her. "It doesn't make you very popular."

"Don't think I wouldn't do it."

"I suspect you'd need a lot more that what you've already got. Especially against George Creighton. He's an old hand."

"Yeah, but…"

"Look," Dave reasoned. "I know why you're really here."

"Do you, now?"

"Yes. You're a good detective. You look around at your team. Everyone's patting themselves on the back over the Leyton Cross shootings. But you know they cut corners on the Lee Royle case. You want this thing solved. Even if the victim was a cop killer."

"But what if it's more than just a matter of cutting corners?"

"What do you mean?"

"Someone's been interfering with this investigation."

"Do you have any proof of that?"

"Well, there's you, for a start."

"I'm not interfering with the investigation. I really am trying to find out who killed Lee Royle."

"Yeah, right. So, who are you working for?"

"That's client confidentiality, I'm afraid."

"That's bullshit."

"Maybe. But what if we worked on this together?"

"You've got to be joking."

"If we teamed up, shared information,"

"That's just not going to happen."

"And if I find something significant, you could take the credit for it."

"I don't think so."

"A career defining case for anyone who managed to solve it."

There was a sparkle in his eye as he looked at her. She held his stare for a moment, then huffed and looked away.

"This is getting us nowhere," she said.

He stood up and handed her a business card. She took it reluctantly.

"And it would be good to have your contact, too," he went on. "You know, just in case anything comes up."

She huffed again and gave him her card. He smiled.

"Think about it," he told her.

And he knew she would, even as she left his office shaking her head. And he might be able to work this to his advantage, he thought. He wondered once more about all of the strange connections that linked to the supposed road rage killing. And spurred on by her own new curiosity, DC Hussain could do some of the legwork for him. Which would give him some time. There was that other thing he had to do for Jo, and that took precedence for the moment. Finding out the truth behind her dark story. The job he had promised he would deal with it personally.

Meera Hussain's mind was racing. She was so tightly wound up when she walked out onto the street that she nearly jumped when she felt her phone go. She pulled out the mobile and squinted at the screen. **No Caller ID**, it read. She swiped to accept it.

"Hello?" she said.

"It's a Mazda MX-5," came a low, flat voice.

"What?"

"The red sports car. It's a Mazda MX-5."

"Sorry, who is this?"

"The eyewitness."

"Wait–"

But the call had already ended. She stopped still in the middle of the pavement and tried to catch her breath.

"Fuck!" she seethed through clenched teeth.

She had an unnerving feeling that she was being played. That she'd found herself in the middle of some kind of elaborate plot, and that she was being set up for something. Something bad. Her rational mind was warning her off, telling her to drop this dangerous obsession with the Lee Royle case. But a deeper instinct was getting the better of that.

She had a lead now. And she was going to follow it.

39

As Kent basked in a sultry July heatwave, a gloom descended upon Sevengates. Fear and suspicion stalking every part of that ill-omened place. As Jo waited to hear back from Dave Shepherd, the confidence she'd had in dealing with the private investigator was undercut by a growing unease.

A sense of a reckoning came closer, and she felt dread of it returning. She knew she should have done something years ago, that now might be too late to find any redemption. She could expect a harsh judgment of her actions. And time would tell it all.

The day passed with deadly momentum and dismal lethargy. Craig wasn't returning her calls, and Jo knew that if things weren't patched up with him soon, all the plans for the drugs consignment coming in to Folkestone could be compromised. Worse still, word of Eddie's treatment of his brother-in-law had got out, treacherous rumours of a deadly rift in the family were starting to spread.

Their legitimate front was also in chaos. Terry Rice had left, and with him went that spark of genius that had given the venture such promise. All his grandiose schemes of making them untouchable now risked becoming a lost dream.

So Jo watched as Eddie brooded morosely, retreating to the darkness of the house as it grew bright outside. Lying in wait, ready to catch her out somehow. She remembered what Shepherd had said when she told him that Eddie had become suspicious of everyone. *Even you?* he had asked. That would make sense, in his paranoid logic, after all.

And she knew that keeping things from him was bound to make him mistrustful. They had become so close in their short time together. So intense. They could read each other's emotions, yet not quite make any sense of them. When she felt Eddie's eyes on her, there seemed no refuge from an accusing gaze. It fed her guilt and made her feel helpless. It was as if he detected some sense of shame in her, some knowledge of her secret.

She wished she could tell him, but once more, she felt she had to wait until she knew it all. Besides, he was in no state to deal with it just now. So she waited, caught up in the remorse for all her years with Lee Royle. With no escape from his murderous legacy, Jo was haunted by his hateful imagination with its morbid superstitions. The killer inside. The blood rival. She felt as damned as he was.

So she too sought sanctuary in the darkness. Somewhere safe that she might comfort Eddie and find solace for herself. A place for them to hide together, where they might be unseen and unknowable. A night that might belong to them.

The eyewitness. Eddie went over it again and again in his self-medicated haze. He had seen something; he was sure of it. In that moment at Junction 1A. It was as if all this time he had been merely looking at something, but suddenly he had looked through it. Some terrible truth was waiting to be revealed. But what?

The details of the murder became clearer, yet something essential was obscured. If only he could clear his mind. Open his perception completely.

The headaches were a block to some hidden knowledge; he knew that now. They stopped him thinking about something. The drugs killed the pain, and for a while they brought strange visions. In their opioid euphoria, he became the eyewitness himself. Seemingly able to channel images of the crime.

But he began to realise that these were mere illusions. And that the drug was soon losing its power to take him to a heightened state. He had already started to feel the agony of withdrawal between doses.

The harsh sun looked down from above, and he felt horribly exposed. The eye of heaven staring in ruthless surveillance, noting every moment. A sky-clock ticking away, so patiently counting the days. That was the true eyewitness.

So he stopped taking the pills and faced the torment in his mind. But he had to get out of the light, to escape its pitiless brightness. To find some illumination within. He imagined himself blind, like Terry Rice. Seeing the unseen.

He lay in bed, shrouded by a single sheet, writhing in a fever dream of combat. Enacting the movements of the men as they fought. Reliving it somehow. No longer seeing it. Feeling it.

The knife came down once more, for the last time, and he lay still. Supine and insensible, dead to the world.

"Eddie," she murmured softly and reached out to touch him.

And he suddenly came to life, his body alert and full of need. He gasped, as if coming up for air.

"Babe," her voice a lustful lullaby.

Jo was above him, naked and kneeling astride him, her hands framing his face. As she touched his neck, there was an exquisite moment when he imagined that she had come to kill him. To put him out of his misery. Instead, she caressed him gently as she slowly lowered her body onto his.

They locked together now in a tight embrace; moved in a slow, insistent rhythm. This was the very heart of their intimacy, beyond doubt, unassailable. This instinct of oblivious bliss they had known from the very beginning. As perfect strangers, when they had been nothing, then everything, to each other in an instant. Then, as now, they pulled each other close, bodies bound together, their love a mortal struggle.

Jo woke early the next morning and was careful not to rouse Eddie curled up next to her. His lower lip quivered; his eyes flickered gently beneath closed lids as he slept. She tried not to think too hard about the dreams he might be having. It was a cool bright morning, and the air was light and fresh. There was a tender sense of hope about the day.

She checked on Annie, who dozed so much more placidly than her father. With precious little memory yet to process, her mind was yet untroubled. Jo gently planted a kiss on her daughter's smooth forehead.

She let Fraser out and watched him eagerly race across the grounds of Sevengates. The sun was already up as she walked out into the garden. But its blaze seemed less angry, more benign than the day before, blessing all that flourished in its tribute. She decided to pick some flowers, to make a kind of offering of her own.

She was arranging a bunch of heavy stemmed blue delphiniums in the kitchen when Eddie staggered downstairs, squinting at something on his smart phone. As he looked up from the screen his face was a haggard scowl.

"Good morning," she said brightly.

"Is it?"

His eyes glared in pain once more. She sighed and reached out to him, but he flinched from her touch.

"What are all these flowers for?" he demanded.

"I just thought–"

"What is it? Has somebody died?"

He let out an ugly laugh.

"Eddie."

"Yeah. Remember that stupid wreath at Lee's funeral? The King of Kent. Is that what you want for me?"

"What?"

"Another wreath. The King must die. Another king dead, another floral tribute. Is that your plan?"

"I don't understand."

"You want me dead; that's what I mean."

"Don't be ridiculous."

"Well, you're up to something, aren't you?"

"No."

"Trying to pin Lee's murder on me."

"Why would I want to do that? It was *you* that was so adamant about the investigation."

"Yeah. Very convenient. You wait for me to do the right thing by you, to find your ex-husband's killer. Then you bring in this private detective. An old friend. Right. I saw how you were with each other. I know what this is all about."

"It's not like that, I swear."

"I'm not fucking blind, you know."

"Please, Eddie."

"Now, you want to put me in the frame for it."

"What?"

"For the murder."

"Look–"

"I know you went to see him. Behind my back."

"What?"

"Jamal saw you. Coming out of his offices in Bromley."

"I was just…" Jo was suddenly flustered.

"You were just what?"

"Going through some details of the case."

"Liar!"

"Eddie, look," she sighed, realising that she had to get things straight, to finally reveal her secret to him. "There's something I've got to tell you."

"For all I know, you and Dave-fucking-Shepherd have been planning this all along."

"It's not like that. But you need to know…"

"Yeah, right from the start. Get rid of Lee and find someone to take the blame."

"Will you just listen for a moment!"

Eddie's phone started ringing, cutting the argument dead. He looked at the screen, frowned, and took the call.

"Yes," he said. "What?"

She watched his face go slack as he listened. His eyes widened.

"Hello, Mum," he said.

Eddie caught Jo's gaze, and his face looked suddenly childlike.

He turned away and listened to the voice on the other end of line. Nodding and humming at intervals, not responding directly, but simply and slowly taking in the news that was being relayed to him. His manner became ever more sombre at each word. There was a pause as the caller finished talking. Eddie let out a long breath.

"Right," he spoke into the mobile. "I'll come over today... I'll phone you on the way...Yeah...Bye."

"What is it?" Jo asked him as he ended the call.

Eddie stared at her with a bewildered look, a shocked half-smile playing on his lips. He shrugged and told her:

"My father's dead."

40

His mind was suddenly clear. Free of pain. Free of drugs. Utterly lucid.

The headaches were gone, and Eddie felt strangely calm and resolute. His mind was clear, his perception finally open and completely aware. He knew that he should be grieving, but, as he drove away from Sevengates, there was only a sense of peace, a euphoric feeling of relief. As if he were in some state of grace. As if he had been gifted some miraculous cure.

And everything was beginning to make sense to him. As he approached Junction 1A once more, he had a sudden moment of absolute clarity. Yes, he thought, this was the crossroads. The place where three roads meet: past, present, future. It all converged, flooding into his consciousness, coming to him like a memory.

And it was a memory. Though it had once seemed like a dream.

No. A game.

Yes. It had all started as a game, after all.

It was that weekend he had no car. He hadn't had a car all week. He had been waiting on Craig to sort out fitting a secret compartment on his new Jeep. Eddie had dropped it off at that garage in West Kingsdown.

He had to rely on lifts or Übers to get around. But he hated that. Eddie loved to drive. Never happier than when he was behind the wheel. Instead, he found himself stuck indoors all day. Playing the racing game Gran Turismo on his PlayStation. Taking too much coke.

It was then that he noticed the red sports car parked on the street outside his flat in Greenhithe. That silly little Mazda MX-5 seemed to be taunting him. And he began to select it as his car to play in the computer game. Even choosing the same colour.

He played for hours on end, going through different track layouts. He liked the real city circuits like New York, Hong Kong, or Seoul Central. Drawn in by a sharp verisimilitude of level design, he became lost in these worlds as he raced through them. Beneath broad landscapes and looming skylines, he chased an endlessly pixelated horizon. A burnt-out brain buzzed with cocaine, and Eddie's mind strayed into alternate realities.

It was in the early hours of Sunday that a crazy idea began to spark from his deranged senses: that the M25 would be the ideal racetrack for him. The very blueprint of his hustling consciousness. He had heard rumours that back in the 1980s, before there were speed cameras, supercar drivers would compete on the orbital motorway. Meeting up at service stations at night to conduct races and clandestine time trials.

In his obsessive mindset, where his lived experience had now become a vast computer game, Eddie began to wonder how long it would take him to complete an entire circuit of the highway. In the hours before dawn, with little traffic on the road, he reckoned that he might do it in less than two hours. Mere speculation quickly became an urgent quest. This was the game he had to win. It was as if beating the clock like this would take him to a higher level, where he might achieve some elevated sense of existence. It was insane.

But there was a clear logic to it. It almost seemed predestined. As with the Gran Turismo console options, he could select his vehicle. So he went outside and broke into the Mazda MX-5, hotwired the little roadster, and set off on his psychotic joy ride.

He designated Junction 1A as the starting grid and finish line. And he calculated that he would have to keep to an average speed of sixty miles an hour. To avoid being caught speeding, he couldn't risk going over seventy. But he would have to push towards that for as much of the route as possible. By four in the morning, with hardly any traffic around, Eddie was hurtling along relentlessly, careening into some sort of trance. Going clockwise, racing against time.

Eddie reached the Watford turn off in less than fifty minutes; it all seemed to be going to plan. But after that, it all became a bit of a blur. Eddie was on autopilot. Completely off his face by now.

He made Junction 1A just after twenty past five. He'd made the whole circuit in one hour, forty-three minutes. Eddie felt triumphant, coming off the slip road as if in some kind of victory lap. He hardly noticed the dark blue Land Rover Discovery as he cut them up.

But as he slowed down at the traffic lights, the Land Rover overtook him, then swerved round to block him in. Eddie got out of the car. Even then, it all seemed some sort of game. And his mind screamed with rage. Road rage.

Eddie sighed as he passed through the junction once more. The scene of the crime. This was the trauma that the neurologist had spoken of. He must have buried it so deep in his consciousness. He'd been in a sort of panic after the event, everything had moved so quickly. He had learned so quickly to detach his mind from violence and death. Finding Brian Colby's bleeding corpse in that house in Notting Hill. Blowing Ray Adams's brain out by the racetrack on the Isle of Man. Shooting those two men at Leyton Cross.

He learnt fast how to become a killer. The first murder had given him the instinct for it, but only because he was able to block it out. Then the rest could be done in cold blood. Without hesitation.

And so he had maintained an amnesia about what had happened. He was in a state of shock when he got back to Greenhithe. He parked the Mazda MX-5 where he had found it, retracing his steps as if going back in time. It was still early, and there was nobody about. In his flat, he took another line of coke and tried to empty his mind. He found that he could convince himself that he had been there all night. He even went back to playing Gran Turismo, as if training his brain that it had all been a game.

Shock. Fear. Then a survival mechanism. All of these elements worked together in a sublime art of forgetting. So he could act without thinking. Become ruthless enough to get to the top.

But he knew now that he wasn't so cold-blooded. That the headaches and the nightmares had been some sort of psychic struggle he was having with himself. They were his conscience.

And perhaps this obsession with the investigation into Lee's murder was simply a subconscious impulse for resolution within himself. And redemption, too. A deep sense of guilt he had hidden away. Not a bad thing, he mused. It made him human.

But it *was* self-defence, he told himself. It was Lee that had the knife, after all. Lee had held the blade and its advantage, but why had he hesitated? Eddie remembered the moment of indecisiveness, that expression of uncertainty on his assailant's face. Was it a look of compassion?

He was heading West now, counter-clockwise on the great orbital motorway. Going back in time, as well as space. Perhaps he could reset his life. His father was dead, and that had somehow freed him from madness.

Travelling homeward, Eddie blinked at tears. Lamenting a man he scarcely knew. A father he had forsaken and shamed. But his wild years were over now. He would become a better person; he was sure of it. He would wrest himself away from the psychotic world he had been caught up in and put all the bad times behind him.

In the meantime, it was imperative that the investigation into Lee's murder be stopped. He would tell Dave Shepherd to drop the investigation, pay him off for his time. He would apologise to Craig, end this feud that threatened their whole family. And he would make things up with Jo. He wasn't quite sure how he would tell her about killing Lee, or how she might react. But he would find a way.

Because family was the most important thing to him now. He had rebelled against his own, but now there was the possibility of reconciliation. With his mother, at least. He wished he had known his dad better. He had always been a busy man; Eddie had hardly seen him as a child. But there would be time to reflect on good memories. To find consolation in normal grief. Of a respectable life cut brutally short. A hard-working man dead of a heart attack at 53. A severe end, perhaps, but after all the murder and bloodshed Eddie had been witness to recently, a natural death almost seemed a kind of respite. This was an ordinary tragedy.

And it would give him another chance with his mother. To say sorry for all the trouble he had caused them. To explain, somehow, that he had been driven by some destructive urge to follow chaos and disorder. Now he felt that a curse on his life had been lifted, that there was hope for a good life after all. He would tell her that he had made something of himself and become a father. Yes, here, at least, there was some redemption in death. A sense that a bloodline might be continued.

41

It took him just over an hour to get to Potters Bar, to the semi-detached mock-Tudor house where he had spent the first seventeen years of his life. He walked up to the familiar front door with the stained-glass fanlight, he rang the bell and a woman came.

"Eddie," she said cautiously.

"Mum."

Mary Pierce was a strong-featured and austere-looking woman who favoured plain clothes and muted colours. She was wearing a black cotton top and grey trousers. Mourning came naturally to her, thought Eddie.

"Thank you for coming," she said. "I didn't think you would at first."

"I'm so sorry. For everything. I should have…"

He struggled for words, all at once overcome with guilt and remorse.

"Come in." She made a vague beckoning gesture, and he followed her through the hallway.

It struck Eddie then how truly intimidated he had been by his mother as a child. Alienated by her dour and formal manner. His rebellion against her had been of a different nature to that against his father. His dissent with her had been more emotional, visceral.

As a teenager, he had tried to shock her. Winding her up, using bad language, deliberately letting her catch him watching porn on the internet. He had wanted to provoke her somehow, to rouse some kind of passionate response from her. When that didn't work, the really bad behaviour began. By the time he went to prison, he knew that he had truly broken her heart. Now he simply wanted to console the sad woman that had raised him.

They sat in the kitchen together, drinking tea.

"I wasn't a good son," he said. "I know that."

"Eddie…"

"But I didn't mean to hurt you and Dad. It was just…"

"Look," she said. "We need to talk. But I've got so many arrangements to make this afternoon. I'll cook us dinner later. Then, well…"

"Yeah," Eddie agreed. "There are things that need explaining."

"I know. But why don't you have a rest? I've made your bed up. You can stay over if you like. Have a shower or a bath. You know where everything is."

His bedroom was just as he had left it. She had kept his old games console, a stack of magazines, manga comics, and graphic novels. A Tarantino poster still tacked to the wall. He found a box of schoolbooks on the floor, and he absently rifled through them.

He pulled out a small, battered sheet of sugar paper, daubed with lurid poster paint. There were two schematic figures, primitive ideograms of human forms. MUM and DAD were scrawled beneath each of them. Eddie smiled. This was his own work, maybe his first attempt at representation. Like the record of some prehistoric culture, forgotten but preserved somehow.

He scanned the room, with all its trappings of boyhood, and reflected wistfully. He hadn't had an unhappy childhood. He had just been an unhappy child. He wondered why that was.

Lying back on the bed, he checked his phone. There was a missed call from Jamal. He called him.

"All done, bruv," came the voice before he'd had a chance to speak. "Shepherd's premises are all now nicely bugged up. Breaking in was easier than we thought. Guess what his door code is?"

"Listen…"

"1966. You'd think he'd do better than that, ex-copper and everything."

"Forget about putting Shepherd under surveillance, OK?"

"But we just done it."

"I want you to follow up the Folkestone thing instead."

"Right."

"Look, I'm away at the moment. I'll explain everything when I'm back."

He ended the call and found Jo's number.

"Hey," she answered softly. "How are you?"

"I'm all right. I'm going to stay over. Is that OK?"

"Of course."

"Look, I'm sorry."

"What?"

"I've been a nightmare these last few days. Completely out of order."

"Yeah, well."

"Can you forgive me?"

"Babe…"

"This happening has put it all in perspective, you know? Family. That comes first. And we can drop this investigation for a start. I just want us to trust each other."

"Yeah," she said. "I really want that too."

"So, can you apologise to Craig for me?"

"He hasn't been returning my calls."

"Well, try again. Let him know that I accept I'm in the wrong. And that I'll make it up to him."

"I think he'd appreciate that."

"It's going to be all right."

"What?"

"Everything. Everything is going to be all right. I love you, Jo."

"I love you, too."

"I'll call you later."

Eddie switched off his phone and let his head rest back on the pillow. He closed his eyes and let out a long sigh. For the first time in weeks, he felt relaxed without drugs. It was true: everything was going to be all right; he was sure of it. He had reached a place of safety in his life.

He would settle things with Craig. Let his brother-in-law take full charge of all the criminal side of the business while he would concentrate on becoming completely legitimate. He wasn't even sure about Terry's grandiose plans. They had enough capital to sell up and start something smaller for themselves. Then he might spend some time on that charity foundation, make it work as something more than just a PR exercise and money-laundering conduit. Maybe he could do some good in the world. He would have to talk it all through with Jo, of course. He wanted a quiet life and a secure living for his family now, that was for certain. That would be their true kingdom. And he smiled at the thought that he might just become the sort of respectable businessman that would have made his father proud.

Perhaps this was a parting gift, he thought, as he drifted into sleep. His father pointing the way from beyond, saving him from further perdition. His death was a reminder of his own good fortune. And it had awakened a greater awareness. That moment of clarity at the motorway junction. Eddie was a lucky man. He had done bad things, even become a killer. But he had got away with it. Now he knew he just had to be careful.

42

"I should have made him wait in the car. That's what I should have done."

"What?"

"That day I brought Eddie round to meet Lee. I should have made him wait in the fucking car. You do someone a favour and before you know it, they're fucking you over. I was his boss, Jo. His boss. Now, what, I'm supposed to act like I'm his fucking slave?"

Like many quiet men, Craig would really let his mouth run when pushed too far. Jo had known this about her brother for some time. She was just glad that he had finally answered her call. Now she put the mobile on speakerphone and held it away from her face as he unlocked his embittered word-hoard.

"He took advantage and, yeah, I know, I let him. That's the worst of it. A moment of weakness out at Leyton Cross and I let him take over. I didn't expect him to walk all over me. He got my respect. And my loyalty. But those things go both ways. Know what I mean?"

"Yeah, Craig. I do."

"And that business in the lock-up. That was well out of order. But I'm not going to put up with any of this shit anymore. If he wants me as an enemy, that's fine. If he wants a war, I've got plenty of people on my side I could call on."

"What?"

"Because it's not just me. Other people are getting worried."

"Well, I hope you haven't been talking like this to these other people, Craig," she snapped.

He let out a sigh.

"Of course not. I'm not that stupid. It's just…"

"I know. I know. Look, Eddie's said he's sorry."

"Really?"

Craig sounded unimpressed.

"Yeah. And I think he means it. He's been under a lot of stress; you know that."

"That's not an excuse for how he's treated me."

"We'll make it up to you, Craig. I promise. Why don't you come over? We can talk about it properly."

"I don't know. I don't think I'm ready to see Eddie right now."

"He's not here. He's away until tomorrow."

"Where's he gone?"

"I'll explain later. Look…" She suddenly had an idea. "Why don't we go out together?"

"Out?"

"Yeah, out. Have a proper sit down in some posh restaurant."

"Well…"

"Come on. It's been ages since we've had any real time together."

"Yeah. OK. That sounds good."

"Anywhere you fancy, my treat."

"The Ivy in Tunbridge Wells? Give you an excuse to get tarted up."

Jo laughed.

"It's been a while since you've had the chance to do that, sis."

"Yeah. Well, why don't you book it and come and pick me up. You can say goodnight to Annie when I put her to bed."

As Jo ended the call, she felt elated. She felt she was coming out of a dark place into the light once more. This year had been so hard. First the post-partum depression, then Eddie's near madness. But all the bad times of her life could be redeemed by the bright future ahead.

And Annie was on good form that afternoon as they played together. Every gurgle of delight from this happy child told her that she could be a good mother after all.

She felt good about herself as well. She thought of Eddie and how they had made love so ardently the night before. It proved that he still found her a lovable, desirable woman. And as she got ready for the evening, she felt powerful, fearless. She decided to wear her Alaïa Goddess dress in scarlet jersey. A short, sculpted gown with a low neckline and cut-outs on the sides that really brought out her figure in a bold and unapologetic way. She dressed her hair up in a chignon and slipped on a pair of silver Manolo Blahnik stiletto sandals. As a final touch, she pinned on the Stephen Webster Eye of Horus brooch that Eddie had bought her for their anniversary. She looked magnificent.

But as she was about to go downstairs, her phone came to life. Her heart leapt as she saw the name on the screen: **Dave Shepherd.** She grabbed it quickly.

"Hello," she said, catching her breath.

"Jo."

"Yes. What is it?"

She had so many questions, it was unbearable. But there was a pause on the line.

"Hello?" she almost pleaded.

"Look," he said, softly. "We need to take this slowly."

"No," she insisted. "I need to know now."

"OK," he sighed. "You better come over, then."

"Right. Where are you?"

"I'm still at the office. I'll see you there."

43

"I found this."

Eddie held out the painting he had made as a child for Mary Pierce to see as he came into the kitchen. She gasped as she took it, put her hand to her mouth.

"Oh, Eddie."

"Sorry Mum, I didn't mean to upset you."

"It's not that. It's just…"

"I know this is hard for you."

"Yes." She gently placed the picture on the kitchen table. "I only wish…"

She trailed off again, gazing into the middle distance, her eyes filmed with tears. Eddie didn't know what to say. He'd never seen his mother in such a state before. She was usually so controlled. Grief must have hit her very hard, he reasoned.

"I made a lasagne," she went on. "It's in the oven. Shouldn't need more than another twenty minutes. I'll open a bottle of wine."

"Let me do that. Sit down for a bit."

As Eddie uncorked an Argentinean Malbec, he watched her trace a forefinger along the picture. He poured them both a glass and sat opposite her.

"If only you had come back to us," she said. "After Youth Detention."

"The thing is," he sighed, "I felt ashamed. Of what I'd done. Of who I'd become. I felt I had ruined your lives, and I couldn't come back here."

"We might have had a chance, then. To put things right."

"I had become a bad person, Mum. There's no two ways about it."

"It wasn't your fault. Well, not all of it, anyway."

She spoke in such a sombre tone, but at that moment, Eddie felt they were finally on the brink of some sort of understanding.

"We should have done more for you, Eddie."

"No. It's not fair for you to take any of the blame. I don't want that, really I don't. I want to take responsibility for all that I did. Then I can move on. I've already started to do things with my life. I'm a successful businessman."

"So I hear."

"And I've got a wife and child. I know what it is to be a parent. I realise now all the things you and Dad did for me. All the sacrifices you made."

"Well, we tried, but…"

"You should see little Annie," he went on. "She's beautiful."

He smiled at her across the table, all at once proud that he might tell her this joyous news. A beautiful gift, something to balance her grief with joy. This was the cycle of life, after all. The reason for carrying on.

But Mary Pierce's sorrowful countenance did not brighten at this message. If anything, she looked more forlorn than before. He reached out across the table, touched her gently on the arm.

"Mum?" he beseeched her. "You're a grandmother."

"No," she said in a small, quiet voice. "No. Not really."

"What do you mean?"

"Oh, Eddie," she sighed. "We should have told you sooner. I know that now."

"What?"

"When you came home with this" – she picked up the picture – "your dad said we should have told you then. "He's old enough to know, now," that's what he said. But I wouldn't listen, would I?"

"Mum?"

"What was I thinking? Everything we read told us we should have let you know as early as possible. But it got harder the longer we left it."

"What did?"

"So, in the end, it was decided. We planned to tell you when you turned eighteen. But by then you were in Feltham, and you didn't want us to visit. Then you never came home."

"I don't understand. Tell me what?"

"I know, I know. We did the wrong thing. But the thing was, you were so little when you came to us. Only a few weeks old, there wasn't any...what did they call it? Attachment issues. And your birth mother didn't want any further contact, so..."

"Wait a minute...No."

"Yes. Me and your father could never have children. So we adopted."

"I don't believe this."

"You were such a delightful baby. We were so lucky."

"No!" Eddie stood up quickly from the table and his chair toppled backwards onto the tiled floor. Mary Pierce flinched a little then looked up at him.

"I'm so sorry, Eddie," she told him.

"No!" he repeated. "This cannot be fucking true!"

He reached across the table and grabbed at the picture. She cried out as he screwed it up in his hand and tossed it across the room.

Eddie went out to the hallway and put his jacket on, checking the pockets to make sure he had everything he needed. She followed him out and watched as he weighed the car keys in his hand.

"Please don't go," she pleaded. "You're all I have in the world now."

He looked at her mournful face and shook his head slowly. Then he turned and walked out of the front door.

He was soon back on the London Orbital Motorway, driving eastwards, moving clockwise now, as if following some natural order of time once more. Hurtling forwards, into the unknown. He was a man without a past now. What could be his future?

As he caught his reflection in the rear-view mirror, he asked himself: *who the fuck am I?*

It had happened. That dread event his feeling of vertigo had foreseen. All that he had built, mentally and emotionally, a solid tower of self that might reach up to heaven, now came tumbling down. It was as if the earth had opened up to reveal the abyss below. And he was falling, falling.

And the words of Terry Rice came back to taunt him once more. The riddle of life: he had been a fool to try and answer it. He knew now that once you start to solve your own mystery, there is no end to it. You are lost for good. This was the trick of fate, he decided. The whole universe conspiring to send him mad. Everybody he had known had betrayed him. He could trust no one.

Except Jo. As he thought of her, his foot touched the accelerator instinctively. All he wanted at that moment was to bring himself closer to her. She was the one he could truly believe in. She was his only certainty in the world now. Their love was all that he could be sure of.

44

But when Eddie arrived back at Sevengates, Jo wasn't there. As he shouted her name in the hallway, Gabriela came down the stairs.

"Where is she?" he demanded.

"I don't know. Craig…"

"What about Craig?"

"They were going to go out. He was going to come and pick her up. And then…"

"What?"

"She went out on her own."

"Where?"

"She didn't say. She was in a hurry."

He took out his mobile and tried phoning Jo, but the call went straight to voicemail. Something was wrong; he was sure of it. He went down to the basement. Built into the wall behind the stairs was a secret compartment. He unlocked it and took out the fully loaded Beretta 9000 automatic pistol he had acquired for their personal protection.

Then he drove to Bromley. Walked to Dave Shepherd's business premises. Let himself in with the door code Jamal had given him and went upstairs. A light was on in the private investigator's office. Eddie crept along the corridor until he could hear voices. Jo was talking loudly, with a note of panic.

"There must be some mistake," she insisted.

"It's all there, Jo," Shepherd's tone was flustered but placatory. "We can go through it all again if you like."

"But what am I going to do?"

Eddie tiptoed to the door.

"I don't know."

"We've got to do something, Dave."

"What are you suggesting?"

"You've got to fix it, that's what you've got to do.

"How?"

"You've messed with files before. Fix it so it never happened."

"That's not going to be easy, Jo."

"Well, we've got to keep it a secret. We've got to."

The door was partly open now, and he could just about see them both. Dave Shepherd slouched at his desk in a suit and open-necked shirt. Jo was pacing the room, all dressed up for something.

"All this information is confidential," Shepherd told her. "At least you've got that."

"Yeah, but for how long? We've got to stop it."

"Jo…"

"Eddie must never know about this. Never."

Eddie started, as if he was being addressed directly. He pulled the gun out of his jacket and pushed the door open.

"What must I never know?" he demanded.

Jo gasped and Dave Shepherd sat up in his chair.

"Fuck," he muttered.

"Come on," Eddie went on. "What is it?"

The last of the daylight streamed in through the office window, and Eddie squinted against the sun that bled between the buildings of Bromley. He looked at a loose file of papers that spilled out on the desk in front of him. As Dave Shepherd grabbed at an official looking document, Eddie could just make out his name on the top of it. The investigator held the dossier close to his chest, his upper body tense, his face flinching at the automatic that was now pointed in his direction.

"Come on." Eddie beckoned with his free hand. "Give."

"No!" Jo called out. "Don't."

"What?" Eddie turned to her. "What's all this about, Jo? And why are you all dolled up for this fucker? I knew you were both up to something."

"Eddie, please."

He cocked his head towards Dave Shepherd.

"So, what's he found? Let me guess. Some police intelligence report that links me to the killing, is that it? I thought you wanted to pin it on me for some reason, but I couldn't work out why."

"Let me explain something," Jo begged him.

"Because I better see it," Eddie gestured at the document with his pistol. "If they're on to me."

"Who?" Jo frowned.

"The police, of course. Come on" – he beckoned with his free hand – "what have Kent CID got on me?"

"About what?" Shepherd asked.

"Lee's murder. Did you know all along, Jo?" he turned to her. "Or just suspect something?"

"I don't understand," she told him.

"That I killed Lee."

"No," she gasped.

"Yes."

"It can't be. But–"

"I know." Eddie let out a cruel laugh. "I didn't even know it myself. I had a sort of black out. It was a road rage thing, after all. I'd stolen a car, and I was off my face on drugs."

"Wait a minute," Shepherd cut in.

"Yeah, yeah," Eddie was gabbling now, in a manic state. "I tried to have the murder I committed reinvestigated. It's crazy, isn't it? But I was having this sort of selective amnesia. That neurologist I went to see, he said that the brain can play tricks on you."

"No." Jo stared at him, wide-eyed. "I don't believe it."

"But it's true." He turned to face her.

"God," she sobbed. "No."

"What's the matter?" He forced a smile. "I thought you wanted him dead."

"Yeah, but–"

"I didn't set out to do it, Jo. It was self-defence. It was Lee that pulled the knife on me. I just managed to get the better of him. That's all. There was nothing premeditated about it."

"No?"

"No. But maybe it was meant to happen. Somehow."

"Yeah," she sighed. "That too."

"What?" He squinted at her.

"Nothing."

"But the Kent Police were right all along," he went on. "A simple case of road rage. An act of senseless violence, with no real motive. A random thing, you know, like Detective Constable Hussain told us. "The hardest murders to solve." That's what she said. I think we should keep it that way. Now, we've got to cover my tracks."

Eddie face was crazed grin as he nodded at the file Dave Shepherd was still clutching tightly.

"So, let's see what you've got there, for a start. Then you can both explain what the fuck you've been up to."

"Wait," said Jo.

"Come on, hand over what I wasn't supposed to see. What were you going to fix?"

As the gun gestured at his face once more, Dave Shepherd loosened his grip on the sheaf of papers in his hands. He dropped them on the desk and began to slowly slide them across towards Eddie.

"No!" Jo called out.

It was like a cry of pain. Keeping the pistol pointed at the private detective, Eddie turned to face her.

"Please," she pleaded, in a softer tone. "Just listen to what I have to say."

45

"Lee wasn't just a bastard," she said. "He was a twisted bastard. He liked to control people, make them follow his will. He could be charming, sophisticated, but deep down there was real badness in that man. I thought the worst of it was what he did to me, until I heard Chris Ipsworth's story. He grooms the kid, rapes him, then makes him his bitch for life. Sets him up to take the fall for him for that big robbery, and even after eighteen years inside, Chris still couldn't break free of that hold Lee had over him. It was sick.

"Sex and power: it intoxicated Lee. He liked to fuck people over, he really did. And he got away with so much over the years. He was a lucky man, and that made him superstitious. Always on the lookout for some sign or omen. Always ready for the moment when he might have pushed his luck too far.

"Like when he killed that undercover cop. We'd had sex that night, first time in a while. Anyway, he gets arrested straight after the killing, so when he finds out I'm pregnant, he knows it happened that night. Well, he became obsessed. Banged up in a cell and fixated on this idea that he'd become a father and a killer at the very same moment. It was some sort of curse; he was sure of it. 'There's a killer inside of me,' he told me. 'I don't want to pass that on. I don't want a killer for a son. He'd be my blood rival.'"

"The blood rival," Eddie muttered.

"Yeah. Lee was scared of his own flesh and blood. He seemed more worried about that than the murder charge he was facing. So, he made me–" Jo gasped. "He made me get rid of it."

"What? He made you have an abortion?" Eddie frowned.

Jo's eyes widened. She flashed a glance at Dave Shepherd, then back to Eddie.

"Yes," she nodded slowly. "That's what he wanted. A sacrifice."

"That is sick."

"Yeah." Jo let out a bitter laugh. "And when he got off the murder rap, he said to me, "See? I was right. We did the right thing." Like he had made a deal with the gods or something."

"Christ."

"Yeah, like I said, a twisted bastard."

"But what has that got to do with all this?"

"We have to cover our tracks. You were right to kill him, Eddie. Now we have to make sure that nobody else knows about it."

"I don't understand."

"You said yourself: we should finish with this investigation." She gestured towards the paperwork on the desk. "And get rid of anything that might link you to the murder."

"Yeah, but…"

"Please, Eddie. Let's just go home. Dave can be sworn to secrecy about what you did, can't you, Dave?"

"Well…" Shepherd shrugged and glared at the gun.

"We'll make it worth your while, don't you worry." She turned to Eddie. "We can leave it all with him. He can dispose of all the evidence for us."

"But what did he find?"

"It doesn't matter, Eddie. Please, I'm begging you. Let's just go back to Sevengates. We can be happy there, can't we?"

She made a move towards the door.

"Come on," she said. "Let's just walk away."

"I can't do that, Jo."

"What?"

"I need to know."

"Come home with me, babe. Please."

"No."

She was at the doorway by now, staring back at him. Her face stark and empty of expression.

"Then there really is no hope," she sighed. "No chance. It's all over."

Jo turned to leave, then looked back one more time.

"Poor Eddie," she whispered.

And she was gone.

For a moment, he thought about going after her, and telling her that, yes, everything was going to be all right. Instead, he turned back to face Dave Shepherd, levelling the snub nose of the Beretta at the man.

"Look, Eddie…" Shepherd's face cracked into a fearful grimace.

"I want you to tell me what this is all about." Eddie's free hand prodded at the files on the desk.

The private detective looked down the barrel of the pistol, then up at Eddie Pierce.

"You better read it yourself," he said, with as much calm as he could muster. "Take a seat."

The sun had set by now, and as Eddie sat down and picked up the file, he squinted in the half-light to focus on it properly. But he could quickly discern that it wasn't a police intelligence report. It was a local authority social services file from nearly twenty years ago. A sub-heading read: *The Children, Family and Community Services Department*. He leafed through the other papers: a letter of referral from an agency, an assessment certificate, an application form. It took him a while to read through it all and process its dread information. But it all confirmed what Mary Pierce had told him. These were his adoption papers.

And his birth mother was Jo Royle.

He stood up, screwed up his face and let out an animal howl of pain. His hand still gripped the gun, and Dave Shepherd feared for his own life as he watched this young man's torment. But when Eddie opened his eyes once more, he looked right through the man. The eyes were dead as they turned to glare at the darkening sky. Sodium lights were coming on in the street below.

"Let the night come," Eddie muttered softly, and walked out.

46

As soon as Jo got back to Sevengates, she grabbed a half empty bottle of white wine from the fridge in the kitchen and went upstairs to the bedroom. She locked the door and sat on the edge of the bed.

She had thought she might have been able to buy herself some time in telling Eddie the lie about having an abortion. There was some truth to it, after all. This was what Lee had wanted. But it was too late for that by the time he learnt that she was carrying his child. The blood rival that he had feared so much.

Jo reached over to a bedside cabinet and pulled out the boxes of Nortriptyline she had kept there. She had stopped taking the medication for weeks now and had built up quite a supply. Pulling out the blister packs, she started to pop out the orange and white capsules. She began to feed on them absently, chasing down each one with a sip of wine.

It was during a remand hearing that he had told her what to do. They had transferred him from HMP Brixton to the holding cells at Lambeth magistrates court, and she saw him there.

"It's for the best, Jo," he had insisted.

"No."

"Yes. And don't think you're going off to have this kid without me. I'm planning to beat this thing. I'll be back soon enough."

"Couldn't we…?"

"No. You'll do what I say. Remember: you'll never be free of me, even if I do get sent down for life."

"What do you mean?"

"Just do it, Jo. Put the baby up for adoption. I don't want that little time bomb ticking away in my life."

"Christ, Lee."

"I mean it. There's a killer inside of you – well, he will be if *we* bring him up."

"It doesn't have to be that way."

"No? You think you're some kind of fit mother? You're as bad as me, Jo. Don't you forget that. And don't forget that whatever happens to me, I can always keep an eye on you. So, do what you're told. Otherwise…"

And he let the threat of that word hang in the air.

As she left the cell, Ray Spinks was waiting outside. He was a Detective Chief Superintendent back then, already a high-flyer. Here to have a secret meeting about the missing proceeds of the Tunbridge Wells Cash Depot Robbery. And how he might clandestinely help Lee's defence in his impending trial.

Jo was certain that Lee had arranged it so that she would see him with such a powerful man. It was a reminder to her that she would find no protection from the authorities if she went against her husband's word. And all the while, she knew that the control Lee wielded over her was even more ruthless on the other side of the law.

Because every week, a brutal-looking minder would turn up at Sevengates to take her to visit Lee at Brixton prison. Hardly talking as they drove up the A20, but always watching. In the back seat, she'd catch his dull-eyed stare, slotted in the rear-view mirror.

And every week, Lee would chip away at her. With soft-spoken menace, he would undermine her confidence. Find clever ways of making her feel stupid or fearful. Helpless. All done with that smooth smile of his, sugared with sweet words and endearments.

Jo was so young, only eighteen. She still thought of Lee as her first true love. He had charmed her so, right from that first night they had met at Flicks in Dartford. She still imagined that he cared deeply for her, that the quiet fury and intimidation stemmed from some genuine passion he had for her. It was up to her to placate him, to do right by her man.

So she found it hard to stand up for herself, to assert her own true feelings about the baby she was carrying. And along with the threats, it was Lee's appeals to her better nature that helped break her. That it would it be better for her child to be raised in a normal, loving environment. "Do you want the best for them, or just the best for yourself?" he demanded. "Aren't you just being selfish?"

And Jo began to believe that she could never be a good enough mother. And that, like Lee, she was cursed somehow. So she contacted social services and an adoption agency. She felt so trapped by then, and this seemed the only way out.

A baby given up for adoption before its birth is officially known as a "relinquished child", and she remembered shuddering a little at the sad sound of those words. She was told that there was always a demand for the relinquished ones, and that it would not be hard to find a place for hers.

The assessment and referral process all went so smoothly. It was to be a closed adoption, meaning that the birth parents would have no further contact with the child. And it was all dealt with in complete confidentiality. Lee saw to that. Jo had little sense of choice about the matter, and nowhere else to turn to, but she certainly agreed to this part of it. She never wanted anybody to know what she had done.

So she let everything be dealt with around her. She wanted to diminish herself and just let it happen. When she started to show, she hid herself away. Staying indoors, isolated and alone.

She had learnt by then that when men are sent to prison, it is often women who do their time for them. And her pregnancy had now become a legal process, its term grimly shadowed by Lee's impending prosecution for murder.

Jo went into labour on the first day of the trial at the Old Bailey. It was a relatively easy birth. Something she had not quite expected. It was as if she had deserved to feel more pain than she did.

A boy. A beautiful child. Perfect. When she first held him, she felt pure love and overwhelming fear. She didn't have long with him, she knew that. And this would break her heart. She just wanted to know every part of him. His wrinkled face, his tiny fingers. She tried to memorise his scent.

On her last day in the hospital, she lay in bed, her tiny son sleeping on her chest. Her bag was packed, her day clothes on the chair. And she whispered to him: *I love you, but I've got to let you go*. Then she got up, gently placed him in the cot before he could wake up, got dressed and left.

She had confirmed with social services and the adoption agency that she didn't want to know anything about the new family her baby son was going to. She didn't even want to know his name. They offered counselling, but she refused. She didn't want to talk about it. Jo decided the best way to deal with this was to cut herself off completely.

Two days later, she was at the Central Criminal Court to see her husband take the stand. She dressed immaculately, in a dark-blue Chanel suit. She knew that Lee would expect her to look suitably impressive in the visitor's gallery. And her appearance at the trial caused a stir amongst the press; paparazzi buzzed at her as she pushed through the crowd outside the Old Bailey. Her pale face strangely photogenic. She felt raw and empty, like a ghost.

Lee's barrister had already managed to raise serious questions about the operational planning of the surveillance on Sevengates. It was made to seem a bungled affair. Each police statement was meticulously taken apart. With an agile gift of cross-examination, the defence lawyer detailed all the conflicting accounts of the event to expose a sense of official confusion over the matter. All the time, insisting on the one fact that was clear: the undercover officer, dressed in a balaclava and camouflage gear and hiding in the darkness of the grounds, had failed to properly identify himself when challenged by the owner of the house.

Lee had been taken into custody after the killing, and an examination by a police surgeon had recorded marks of a struggle on the prisoner, bruises and a black eye. So when the pathologist appearing for the prosecution took the stand, the defence lawyer carefully nuanced his testimony, making the expert witness appear to confirm that the undercover cop must have struck the accused before he was stabbed.

So when Lee entered the witness-box, Jo noted a quiet confidence in her husband, that he might just get away with his self-defence plea. He had dressed for the occasion, too. In a pale-grey Armani suit and pink paisley tie, he presented himself as a successful businessman foolishly tempted into the fringes of white-collar crime.

He freely admitted to relatively minor charges of money-laundering and tax fraud but insisted that he knew little about the Tunbridge Wells Cash Depot Robbery beyond what he had already told the police. Cooperating with their inquiry had, in fact, put him in fear of his life. And on the night of the killing, he had thought that the hooded man in his garden was a hitman sent to keep him quiet. It was a consummate performance.

It took the jury twelve hours and thirty minutes deliberation to reach their verdicts. Lee was found not guilty of murder by a ten-to-two majority. There was a unanimous decision of guilty on the other charges. He graciously thanked them from the dock, then turned to look up at Jo. He winked and blew her a kiss. She suddenly felt sick and fled the visitor's gallery.

The women's toilet seemed a quiet refuge from the tumult that had erupted in the courtroom. But for a slight figure bent over the sink, sobbing. She looked up as Jo entered. The mirror framed the tear-streaked face of the young widow.

"Oh," Jo murmured. "Oh. I'm so sorry."

The woman's reflection glared at her in the glass, all at once recognising the wife of her husband's killer. She scowled.

"I don't want your pity," she spat the words. "You bitch."

Lee was sent down for a seven-year sentence and ended up serving five. Jo was on her own for a while, though she was never entirely free of Lee Royle. Forever marked by his legacy, she knew there was no escape now. The day after the verdict, *The Sun* ran the story on page five with a photo of her looking stony faced outside the Old Bailey. NO REMORSE, read the tagline: *stylish but cold Jo Royle watches her cop-killing husband dodge justice.* She felt frozen in that image, the cold bitch that didn't care.

And she came to accept what Lee had told her, that she was as wicked as he was. She became hardened, finally believing they had done the right thing, after all. They were bad people, and their baby would have grown up to be bad too. It was a good thing that the child had got away from their hateful world.

Jo slipped another pill in her mouth and took another sip of wine. She had nearly swallowed a whole packet of the anti-depressants now, but she had to do this slowly. She didn't want to retch. She took a breath, then continued.

The medication was for clinically diagnosed post-natal depression, of course. But the real cause of her deep melancholy after her daughter's birth had been the sickening fear that her baby would be taken from her once more. She couldn't bear the thought of going through all that again. So she hoped that the anti-depressants might work permanently now. To cure her grief for good.

And the drugs had already begun to take effect. Her mind reeled with sadness, with madness. It would all be taken away from her once more. They would come for Annie just as they had for her first child.

Eddie.

Oh, God, she thought. Her dear sweet baby was Eddie. The lost child she had hired Dave Shepherd to track down.

She had already found him. Her one true love that had come to her after all those heartless years with Lee.

She thought Eddie had saved her from the curse of her life, but he was part of that curse himself. All of Lee's worst fears had been realised. The killer inside had murdered him after all. The blood rival had come to take his deadly revenge.

And she, too, faced terrible vengeance. There was no one left to blame but herself. She should never have gone along with Lee's paranoid scheme; she was now as guilty as he was.

But what a cruel fate for Eddie. The poor boy had been fitted up by destiny. What would he do when he found out the truth? He would hate her. Yes. Despise her. She couldn't bear that.

And the whole world would be disgusted by how they had loved each other. She wondered grimly what the tabloids would make of it all. Little Annie would be made to suffer, that was for sure. Their daughter would be made to carry this awful burden.

As Jo pulled out another foil strip she felt a darkness flooding into her mind. She had taken enough; she knew that now. She sighed as she rolled onto the soft mattress. This was where it would end, she decided, on this cursed bed. Where both of her doomed children had been conceived. She heard Daniela's frantic voice calling to her, banging on the door.

Her last thoughts were of Eddie. Her partner in crime. Yes. It had been a truly shocking offence they had committed together, but it had been so wonderful. She smiled as she swooned into a big sleep. Everyone would condemn them for what they had done, but it had been beautiful. Pure bliss. A love that was wrong, yes, so wrong. But true.

47

Born to lose.

That's what Eddie thought as he gazed in horror on Jo's lifeless form. Her skin so pale against the scarlet gown. She looked at peace, eyes closed, lips gently parted. Just a chalky trace at the corner of her mouth.

He had come back to the house in a murderous rage. Shouting for Jo as he stormed up the stairs, gun in hand. He kicked at the door in until it broke from its frame and toppled in with a lumbering swagger. Still raving, he steadied himself, wild eyes scanning the room. Then he froze as he saw her lying so still. A mortal silence descended over Sevengates.

As he approached the bed, he caught sight of the opened boxes of pills, the plundered foil and plastic packs, the empty wine bottle on the bed. He reached out to gently touch her face. Her flesh was still warm, but there was no movement in her body. *No*, he thought, *no*.

She looked so serene. Like a queen lying in state. The marriage bed now a funeral bier. His very existence was a cruel trick, he thought. He'd once imagined himself lucky, but life was a losing game.

Born to lose.

He had finally solved the mystery. The riddle of life Terry Rice had warned him of. And though he had thought he had chosen a life of crime, it had chosen him. He had been marked down from birth. He had always been part of the badness.

He knew who he was now. What he was. The blood rival.

A father killer.

A motherfucker.

He gasped and looked down at Jo once more. His lips quivered and he could not stop them uttering that primal murmuration.

"Mum," he mumbled, then clapped a hand to his mouth.

As if to stop the fearful word.

No, this was too much to bear. He wanted no longer to speak or hear or see. He screwed up his eyes, wishing he could obliterate all his senses.

But he could not look away. He opened his eyes again and looked down at the only person in the world who had ever really meant anything to him. His only love.

Time had found them out. That vigilant enemy that spares no one. Time the accuser, watching patiently on us all. He longed to hide from the light of time, to share her sightless sleep and live in darkness.

He traced his fingers along her face, her neck, the shallow notch of her sternum. He touched the red dress that shrouded her. God, she was beautiful. His knuckles brushed against the Horus brooch.

And it seemed to glare up at him, mockingly. Another eyewitness to their crime.

Yes, he saw it all now. That time is the all-seeing eye, unblinking in its judgment. And he had seen too much, he thought, as he began to unfasten the jewelled clasp.

He looked at her once more, taking one last glance.

Yes, he had seen enough. Now he might find refuge from the agony of perception. He would not miss much; he was sure of that. He comforted himself with the fact that he would not have to look upon the world ever again. Then he pulled out the long pin of the brooch and brought it up to his face.

48

Craig swerved to let an ambulance pass, then continued up the drive towards Sevengates. There were several police vehicles, and another ambulance parked up outside, people in hi-vis jackets coming to and from the house. A short-haired woman in plain clothes was standing by the front door. As he approached on foot, a uniformed officer tried to bar his way.

"I'm family!" he shouted at them.

The woman came over and flashed her ID at him.

"Detective Constable Hussain," she said. "Who are you?"

"Craig Cadmoor," he replied. "Jo Pierce's brother."

"Right." She nodded at the uniform. "Let him through."

"What the fuck's happened?" he asked as he followed her into the hallway.

"Can I ask what your business was here, tonight?"

"I was supposed to be taking Jo out. Then I get a message that she couldn't make it. I tried to call her back, but she didn't answer. I started to get worried, to tell you the truth. Fuck, it looks like I was right to."

He caught sight of Eddie sat on a chair, being attended to by two ambulance men. He was an awful sight. An anguished face masked in blood. The darkened eye sockets seemed to dart about helplessly, as if trying to focus on a

void. The paramedics tried to clean him up and apply a loose
dressing.

"Where's Jo?" Craig asked him.

"She's dead." Eddie replied. "An overdose."

"Is that true?" Craig turned to DC Hussain.

She shrugged.

"All I can confirm is that she's been taken to St Mary's in
Sidcup. In that ambulance you passed on your way in."

"Fuck." He turned to Eddie. "And who did this to you?"

"I did."

"What?"

"I just couldn't bear to look any more."

"Christ, Eddie."

"I'm sorry, Craig."

"Sorry?"

"For accusing you. I was wrong."

"Yeah, well…"

"And for all the others I tried to put the blame on. Deep
down, I knew all along who did it."

"Wait a minute," Meera Hussain interjected. "It was you
that phoned me, wasn't it? About the Mazda MX-5?"

"Yeah."

"Why did you do that?"

"I don't know. Everything was so fucked up in my head.
I even thought that *I* was the eyewitness at one point." He
laughed bitterly. "Not much of an eyewitness now, am I?
Did you manage to trace them?"

"The eyewitness?" Meera asked.

"Yeah."

"Not yet."

"Well, you won't need them now. I can solve your murder
for you."

"Really?"

"Yeah. I did it."

"What?"

"It was me. I killed Lee."

"Wait a minute, mate." Craig glanced over at the detective constable. "Don't say anything just yet."

"Oh, there's worse to come," Eddie muttered grimly. "You'll soon know it all."

"I'm telling you, let's get you a lawyer first. Before you make any statements."

"No need for that. I admit it. I admit it all. I want to go away, Craig. Go away for a long time. A proper stretch inside, that's what I need. I don't want to see anyone. And I don't want anyone to see me. But there's just one thing. A favour."

"Name it."

"Look after Annie. She's going to have to deal with a lot when she grows up. I want you to protect her as much as you can."

"Of course."

"You promise?"

"Yeah, of course."

"Where is she?"

Craig could see Gabriela nearby cradling the child in her arms. He beckoned her over and got her to crouch down with the baby as Eddie reached out. Annie curled her tiny hand around one of his fingers.

"Oh, Annie." Eddie sighed.

He kissed his daughter's hand then let it go. Meera Hussain stepped forward.

"Edward Pierce, I'm arresting you for the murder of Lee Royle," she said, putting her hand softly on his shoulder.

"You do not have to say anything, but it may harm your defence if you do not mention when questioned something which you later rely on in court. Anything you do say may be given in evidence."

The paramedics helped him up, but as he began to shuffle towards the front door, he suddenly turned and called out:

"Annie! Oh, God, Annie!"

"Come on, mate."

"No!"

He grabbed blindly at Craig, pulling him close.

"Listen," Eddie hissed. "Listen."

"No, mate." Craig unclasped the hands that clawed at him. "You listen. You've got to go now."

"But, but..."

"Yes! You don't give me orders now," he whispered intently. "You're not the guvnor anymore."

As they led him out, Craig turned to Meera and pointed at his own eyes.

"So, that was self-inflicted?"

"Yeah."

"That's fucked up. This whole thing's fucked up."

"That's one way of putting it," she agreed.

"Christ knows what people are going to make of all this."

They watched as Eddie was helped into the waiting ambulance.

"What do you think?" she asked him.

"Be lucky," he whispered under his breath.

"What?"

"That's what guys in my kind of game say to each other: be lucky. Like it's the only advice worth giving. Be lucky. Lee used to say it a lot, and he was a lucky bastard. For a while, at least. And you know, I once thought Eddie must have been the luckiest man alive. He had it all, you know? And at such a young age, too. But, well, too much, too young, as they say. It can all get taken away, just like that. Just goes to show: no one can call you lucky. Not really. Not until you're dead."

49

Jo was in the Underworld. It took her a while to realise that she was in some sort of suspended animation, deep beneath the surface of the Earth. She remembered a school trip to the Chislehurst Caves, when Craig had tried to scare her as they were led though the chalk maze of ancient mining tunnels.

"If you get lost down here," he had warned her, "the ghosts of the dead will come and get you."

But it was not fear that she felt now, nor any other strong emotion. Just an overwhelming sense of lethargy. Death was so tiring. She was exhausted.

And the house of the dead was a curious place. It seemed much like that mortuary where she went to identify Lee's body. Except that it went on and on, stretching out in every direction. An infinity of tiled rooms and corridors with fluorescent strip lighting. Trolleys ferried dead souls through swing doors, each to their assigned slab to lie in eternal post-mortem.

She could not move, but she had a kind of awareness that hovered above, looking down at her surroundings. The corpses close to her all appeared to be those she had known or been connected with. Lee was there, of course, looking as imperious as she had left him. So was the undercover cop that her husband had stabbed to death all those years ago. Brian Colby was nearby, his dead finger still pointed at the book by John Donne and its conundrum. Ray Spinks stared out at oblivion with a shocked look on what remained of his face, forever held in that moment when he realised he had been caught out. And Chris Ipsworth's doomed expression watched mournfully, his chest riddled with bullet holes – *Why did they always say "riddled"?* Jo wondered sleepily. *Is everything a riddle?*

They all seemed neatly autopsied, their wounds cleaned and sewn up, their bodies somehow preserved. A delicatessen aura hung in the air. The scent of dried flesh, cured meat. And a briny flavour parched her lips. It was so thirsty in hell.

Once, she heard the stern clip-clop of leather-soled shoes on the tiled floor. It was Terry Rice, as dashing as ever in a velvet-collared frock coat and a paisley cravat. A dandy in the underworld. And with a cadaverous charm that did not look out of place.

"Are you dead, Terry?" she asked him.

"No, but you know me. I like to go below the surface, into the unconscious."

"Even down here?"

"Oh, yes. I'm access all areas, darling. And I get some of my best tips down here. Whoever said the dead don't tell tales was a big fat liar. That's all they do, you know. Information: that's what remains of us. That's all we really leave behind."

She tried to talk to him, there were so many things she wanted to ask, but he was in a hurry. He had a meeting with a soldier on his way back from some Middle Eastern war, wanting advice.

"Wait," she said, but his footsteps were already an echo in a distant corridor.

There were other visitations, but none quite so vivid. Dim shadows came and went. Distant voices imploring her, asking questions, demanding knowledge of the afterlife.

She recalled going with a friend to a psychic meeting in Thanet. A woman claimed to be a medium, able to contact the spirits of loved ones that had passed away. She spoke in tongues that droned answers to eager audience members in the crowded community centre. Now Jo thought that she might be the subject of some sort of séance herself. She had a growing feeling that her brother was trying to get in touch with her from the other side. But the voices, though insistent, sounded vague and unintelligible, as if *they* were the ghosts. It is the living that haunt the dead, she thought.

Then there were lights in her eyes. Her eyelids were pulled back in turn, and she was dazzled with a sudden brightness. She found she could move her fingers a little. And the twitching of her hand seemed to conjure something.

"Look!" came a voice. "She's moving!"

There was a sudden sense of clamour around her, yet a calm stillness within. Then she began to float, rising to the surface of consciousness, her senses stirring. Painful feelings returned to her numbed body. Emotions.

She wasn't ready for this, she told herself. She wasn't ready to once more face the madness she had tried to block out by killing herself. She knew now that she was coming back to life, and the thought of that terrified her.

As blurred figures flickered to and fro around her, she realised with dread that she would now have to try to make sense of things. Craig's was the first face fully focussed.

"Hey, sis," he whispered, with that stupid grin that always made her smile. "You're back."

He explained that the overdose had put her in a coma, but she was now expected to make a full recovery. He sat at her bedside and held her hand.

"Eddie?" she asked.

"Oh, god," he sighed.

"Tell me."

"He's blind, Jo. He blinded himself."

"Fuck."

"Yeah."

"Where is he?"

"On remand. In Belmarsh Hospital Wing. They've got him under observation. He had some sort of memory blackout over Lee's murder. Dissociative amnesia, they call it."

"You've seen him?"

"He doesn't want visitors. He's making a long confession, a long list of things he wants taken into consideration."

"Shit."

"He's keeping us out of it, though. That's one thing, at least. He just keeps saying he wants to go away for a long time."

In the days that followed, Jo didn't know what to think. The guilt she felt was almost unbearable, but she would have to find a way through; she knew that now. Suicide wasn't the answer. She didn't have to die, not yet. But she would have to find a way to live.

And it was not going to be easy, that much was certain. She deliberately kept away from social media and the news, but she knew that within days the story of her and Eddie had gone viral. It had become a global sensation. Her life would always be a colossal scandal, a public outrage.

And she tried to reconcile the love she had known. The brief and happy life that she had had with Eddie. What would they mean to each other now? And how might she approach him as he retreated into some terrible exile from the world. Eyeless in Belmarsh. What a grim fate for her beautiful Eddie.

On her third day of consciousness, Craig brought Annie in. Jo suddenly felt scared as her brother handed the baby to her. How on earth was she supposed to protect this little one from all the trials and tribulations ahead? This poor child would have to bear the terrible stigma of her origin.

At first, Jo was reluctant to look into Annie's wide-eyed stare, somehow fearful that she might detect some trace of judgment or censure in her daughter's eyes. With what Annie faced in her life ahead, she would have every reason to blame her mother for such ill fortune, after all.

But, of course, she saw no such thing on that innocent face. Only the expression of happy recognition and unconditional affection.

It was far too precious to call hope yet, but it was a look of love. And that's all they needed for now.

ACKNOWLEDGEMENTS

My love and thanks to all my friends and family for being so good to me as I wrote this book; and for the support, solidarity and sheer generosity of so many fellow writers, in particular: Tariq Goddard, Catherine Johnson, Joe Penhall and Penny Pepper.

Thanks to Gemma Creffield, Daniel Culver, Vikki Scott and all at Datura Books; and to Jonny Geller and Ciara Finan at Curtis Brown for keeping the faith, and always giving the best advice.

But the biggest acknowledgement must go to the source of this tale. To Sophocles and his telling of it, and for Greek culture that has done so much to enrich our own. I give humble thanks for what I have borrowed, and sincere apologies for what others have stolen. The true crime story is a mystery of loot stashed in a neo-classical warehouse in London. The denouement is simple: the Parthenon sculptures should be returned to Athens forthwith.

DATURA BOOKS
catering to the armchair detective,
budding codebreakers, the repeat
offender and an emerging younger
readership.

Check out our website at
www.daturabooks.com to see our entire
catalogue.

Follow us on social media:
Twitter @daturabooks
Instagram @daturabooks
TikTok @daturabooks